SEEKING LYDIA

Seeking LYDIA

CHRISTINA HUVELLE

For Mom,
who shared our beloved family with me,
and who demonstrated how fun
digging around in the family roots can be.
More than tongue can tell.

Contents

To everything there is a season,
and a time to every purpose under the heaven:

A time to be born, and a time to die;
a time to plant, and a time to pluck up that which is planted;

A time to kill, and a time to heal;
a time to break down, and a time to build up;

A time to weep, and a time to laugh;
a time to mourn, and a time to dance;

A time to cast away stones, and a time to gather stones together;
a time to embrace, and a time to refrain from embracing;

A time to get, and a time to lose;
a time to keep, and a time to cast away;

A time to rend, and a time to sew;
a time to keep silence, and a time to speak;

A time to love, and a time to hate;
a time of war, and a time of peace.

ECCLESIASTES 3:1-8
KING JAMES VERSION

Lydia

MORE THAN TONGUE CAN TELL

Three hot, golden-topped loaves of bread that I lined up on the kitchen table to cool made me think of my three little girls lying side by side out back under the generous weeping willow. But those girls weren't hot anymore. Their bodies were as cold as the Nebraska soil that was packed in tight around them.

I wiped my hands on the long work apron that was tied around my thick waist. My mouth watered at the rich, yeasty smell, but eating was the last thing on my mind. I pushed open the groaning screen door with my hip and stepped off the porch into our yard.

Oliver had rigged the screen door hinges so they would close automatically, and the wooden frame struck the door jamb once as it shut behind me and then again as it bounced from the force. Although I had a lot to get done, I was distracted and drawn to the distant edge of our farm where our three daughters awaited a visit from their mother.

Unrestricted now by the walls of the house that closed in on me, my view no longer limited by the window frame above the kitchen sink, I could see the whole of the dark gray sky.

The air didn't change much, going outside. Sweat still ran down my back from the humidity that never allowed me to get dry. The thick atmosphere held a heavy mid-summer storm that was ready to break open at any moment, and it didn't let me catch my breath. The constant aching in my heart from the burden of grief and longing for my little girl, Gracie, was also ready to spill forth with the welling emotion that came up so suddenly. It took my breath away to an even deeper degree so I felt I was gasping.

It was 25 years earlier, in 1886, when we buried our first-born, 10-month-old Jessie. When Bessie was born four months later, we never dreamed we'd be laying her next to her sister at just a year and a half. Gracie was our last born, our tenth child. We thought after our seven other children had survived, that God might let us keep her, too. He did, until she was five and a half.

I fished a handkerchief out of my apron pocket. It was one Mama had embroidered for me when I was a girl. White cotton with plain edges held down by tiny regular stitches, with dainty pink flowers in the corner, it was soft, worn from years of use and washing. I used it now to wipe the beads of sweat that tickled my face as they rolled lazily down my hairline and along the bridge of my nose. My tears would run faster, so I held on to it in my fist.

I bent to pick fresh wildflowers along the edge of the path that Oliver and I had worn over the years of comings and goings to visit our daughters where they lay. I always brought something for my girls: pure white prairie larkspur and beardtongue for our sweet Jessie, bright yellow black-eyed Susans and orange desert globe mallows for our fiery Bessie, and the spiderwort and leadplant blossoms that matched our pretty Grace's big blue eyes. Oliver always brought them all pink phlox and coneflowers.

As I approached the graves, I noticed him squatting over Gracie's. Oliver cradled his head in one of his big hands while his other hand lay on the fresh little mound of earth in front of the wooden cross our oldest son, James, had made just two months before. I ducked under the long arms of a willow tree and peeked around the trunk to watch him. The low sound of water running past in the narrow creek on the other side of the tree line was loud enough that he apparently hadn't heard me coming.

He rose, wiping his face with his crumpled handkerchief. His worn denim working overalls hung loose around his long, thin frame. He placed his sweat-stained hat on his head and exhaled loudly, as if blowing out the candles on his birthday cake. He shoved his hands in his pockets as he turned and walked back toward the barn, head down, shoulders drooping.

He hadn't seen me, and since he seemed like a stranger to me, I said nothing to him.

I stayed where I had hidden myself and sank to the ground, sheltered by the long arms of leaves that touched the ground all around me. Knowing no one was around to hear me, I cried for all I had lost, deeply sobbing, until no more tears would come.

For a week after we buried Grace, I could barely speak because of the invisible vice-grip that seemed to have a firm hold on my throat. Oliver did not speak either, and contrary to his comforting custom of wrapping his arms around me as we went to sleep, he turned and faced the wall, his back to mine. I felt so far away from him even though our backs heated one another through the night.

I didn't reach out for him because I didn't care about anything other than my dead child. If she couldn't fill my arms, I wanted nothing and no one else in them. Shards of my broken heart pierced my insides and sent stabbing pain through my chest. I was trying to catch my breath, and somehow hold on despite the feeling that the ground had fallen away from beneath me. I wished the sensation that I was plummeting into a bottomless pit would stop.

My foundation returned when Oliver finally embraced me again. It was like a balm on my soul to feel that physical connection, but we never talked about her. We never shared the depth of our grief with one another.

He went on with his business of growing corn and I went on with mine of keeping house and tending to the garden. We barely spoke her name. I was glad to see Oliver out there at Gracie's grave that day, crying. It made me see that he did care, but how long before he stopped going?

I often felt he had forgotten all our lost girls: Jessie, Bessie, and now Gracie, moving on to leave me alone in my heartbreak.

Grace's high-pitched giggles rang out in my mind as I watched the now-adolescent cats race through the kitchen. She loved nothing better than kittens. From the moment I said it was OK for her to bring them from their mother's nest in the barn to the nest she made for them behind the kitchen stove, her face was alight with wonder and delight at their antics.

"Oh, Mommy, it's so soft and sweet," she told me as she cupped a tiny kitten to her cheek. Its pink mouth was mewing, and its round eyes were open wide.

"Yes, love, now put it down. It wants to run and play."

She did as she was told, and the kitten joined its two siblings on wobbly legs and pounced and rolled and hopped. They practiced their hunting techniques, swatting and softly biting and holding each other with front paws while kicking with back paws. Grace dragged yarn on the floor, and they chased it until they were so tired that they fell asleep right in their tracks.

Grace would then scoop them up and cuddle them under her chin.

"Come feel them purring, Mommy!"

I went to put my hands on the warm furry bodies vibrating 'round my youngest daughter's neck, but what I really wanted to do was kiss her sweet face, cheeks flushed with laughter and blonde tendrils framing her shining blue eyes.

So now, those same kittens continued to grow, but my Gracie's life was done. Her laughter was silenced forever except in my memory, and the presence of the cats was bittersweet. I shooed them out of the kitchen and shut the screen door behind them.

I wanted to do nothing but sit and rock in the chair I'd cradled my babies in and look out at the wide sky that seemed closer to my little girls than I could get. Oliver rarely just sat and gazed on that same sky. I knew as well as he did that the farm wouldn't wait. The garden and the fields had to be weeded, the crops had to be harvested, the chickens had to be fed, and the cows needed to be milked. Every day.

Life went on, as it must, after we buried little Grace, but the presence of our children still at home was a comfort to me. Our youngest boys, Billy and Stubb, were too young to be very helpful on the farm when they were not at school, but old enough to understand our family's loss. They were especially loving in the weeks after Gracie's funeral and would stop for just a moment to plant a wet kiss on my cheek or roughly pat my hand as they ran chasing each other in the front door and out the kitchen door.

Our older children, Lee and Belle, were able to contribute more. Belle helped me with the evening chores after she came home from school, and with the laundry and in the garden on the weekends. She would be fourteen later in the year. Lee was eighteen, and had completed the sixth grade, before he put his studies aside to help Oliver on the farm when our older boys left home to find their own way in the world.

Our first born, James, married Mabel Fuller when he was 23 and already had his own farm. Our second son, Ernest, had more of a wandering spirit. He went west to Colorado and ended up working for pay on another farm, which Oliver would grumble about when he thought he was alone in the barn.

"Ungrateful boy. Off to make some other man's farm better, but can't even help his own Pa keep up his own farm. We're struggling here, and he's off making money. What good is money when you can't spend it anyway? No time off, and nowhere to go anyway. Miles from any city. Not sending any of it home. What's the point? Coulda had this farm if he'd helped me out some, but no—he's got to go off to work some other man's land. Thinks he's going to buy his own farm? Good luck with that! Too much money needed for that. Where you gonna get your tools? Think those plants just sprout outta the ground? Seeds cost money. Fertilizer costs money. He don't know nothin'. Coulda had this farm—if only he'd a stuck around—but no. Some people have to roam the Earth."

"Who's roaming the Earth, Ollie?" I handed him a glass of cool cider.

"No one, Lydia."

"Are you griping about Ernest again?"

"No."

I looked at him like I knew better.

"Boy off and left his own father and brothers to see about the family farm to work some other family's farm. Makes no sense a' tall. Might as well be home in the bosom of his own family. But he always was the ornery one. Just like an old billy goat."

"Apple doesn't fall far from the tree, Ollie. Maybe he needed to see who he was as a man away from home."

"I figured it out at home."

"Well your father let you do that—he left us to go live somewhere else with his new wife, remember?"

"Oh, right. I do remember."

"You figured out how to become a man because your father was a good example for you, like you've been a good example for our boys, Ollie. Now you have to let them become men. Let them have their independence."

"Well, you may be right, Lydia."

"Look at James. He's a good man with a wife and a farm. They are doing so well. That's because you taught him well."

"James was always easy. Ernest was always a fight."

The two never saw eye to eye, but I didn't doubt that our second-born son loved us. He must have had a bigger dream for his life than the small patch of earth that was our farm. He wanted to leave the Nebraska state boundaries.

In fact, Oliver was beside himself when we got the postcard in June 1918 that let us know Ernest had up and joined the fight against the Germans. On the front of the card was a very handsome photograph of Ernest in a military uniform and on the back, he had written, "Dear Mom and Dad + all, I am off to fight the Huns. I'll write from France. I love you all. And don't take no wooden nickels. Love, from Ernest."

"The boy's gone and done it now." Oliver was pacing the kitchen, looking at the postcard where he'd thrown it down on the kitchen table. "He's going over there to get himself shot, or worse, maimed."

"He'll be all right, Ollie. You know he can always get out of a scrape."

"He's done it just to spite me. And his grandfather. Father left Germany to avoid becoming cannon fodder, and now our son has gone running to the battle. To fight against the Germans. We are German."

"No, WE are American. Ernest is American, Oliver. Your father left Germany behind when he came here. He cut all ties with Germany. He learned English, took an American name, and became American so there would be no question what his children were."

Oliver nodded his head, but he said no more about it. I put the postcard away so he wouldn't have to see it and be reminded. There was enough anti-German sentiment in the country during World War I that I didn't want to remind anyone who might have forgotten that my father-in-law's accent was from Central Europe, home of the infamous Hun. We were so grateful when Ernest returned home safe, and he waited until the ripe old age of 33 before he married Mabel Jepsen.

Our oldest daughter, Vinnie, got married to Walter Hans, and they lived in town, where she kept house and Walter drove a truck for a garage. Years later, they would move away with their children to Alliance in the western part of the state.

We followed them, along with James and his Mabel, who for some reason, would never be blessed with children. They seemed content and loved each other beyond reason throughout their marriage. My oldest son and his wife were the best of friends even though their lives were shadowed by a void, an emptiness that somehow echoed my loss—my loss of what I once had, and their loss of hopes that were never fulfilled.

Oliver Franklin and I had a large family together, which was natural to us, since we had each come from fairly large families. Oliver was one of five children, and I was one of eight.

It wasn't long after my older brother, Hi, married Oliver's older sister, Dora, that they went off and started their own farm. Oliver came by on his horse looking for work around our farm. Being short of hands, Pa had him help a bit any time Oliver's own father could spare him, and then during harvest time.

My little brother, George, was of no help, being only five. Our sister, Minnie, who was just eight years old, and I were more helpful to Mama in the house, especially looking after our little sister, Lunetta Grace, who was very busy toddling about and getting into everything.

After a few years, I began to take notice of Oliver. He was respectful to Mama, always calling her ma'am and taking off his hat in her presence. Oliver always put in a good day's work for Pa. He'd tousle the little ones' hair as they ran chasing each other around him. His deep voice was soft when he harnessed up the horses to drive them out to the fields. His blue eyes took my breath away when he leveled them at me, holding my gaze as he greeted me or said good-night when he left to go home.

Oliver's family had moved to Iowa when we were young. Our fathers became acquainted at Grange functions, both political and social. Our families grew close, even closer when Hi and Dora got married.

I could tell that Oliver had a crush on me before I had time to even take notice of any of the other boys in the county. When I was fourteen, during his third harvest season helping Pa, Oliver sought me out in the barn at milking time.

"Lydia?" Oliver's deep voice softly reached out to me from the barn threshold.

I heard the approach of four huge, metal-shod feet and two large, boot-shod ones coming down the aisle toward me. I looked over my right shoulder just as he peered into the milking stall at me. He held Big Blue by the harness, and once he saw me, he continued walking to the next stall.

I heard a pile of hay drop to the floor and then air pulled in and then blown out of the horse's nostrils as he inspected his supper. Blue's soft lips found the sweetest spot and his big teeth crunched on the dried clover and Timothy grass. The workhorse exhaled a contented sigh as Oliver ran the sweat scraper, curry comb, and then the hard-bristled brush rapidly over Blue's body. The four wide hooves each dropped with a thud as Oliver checked them carefully for rocks and thorns from the fields they had walked to plow that day. Oliver took special care with Pa's horses so they'd work hard for him. He knew Pa couldn't afford to have them go lame from standing on anything even as small as a pebble.

I continued the rhythmic pull from Dot's udder. The pail balanced between my feet. I leaned my tired body into her warm one. I closed my eyes and breathed in deeply. The scent of fresh air and manure radiated off her.

It felt like she was nearly done. It was important to get every last drop so Dot's milk wouldn't dry up and leave the family without. My oldest sister, Clary, had let that happen years ago, and the family had never let her forget it even though most of us weren't even born yet. We laughed about it now, but when it happened, it put our Ma into quite a bind, as she tried to find a generous neighbor with a good milker to make up for the loss.

I stood up and quickly moved the bucket out of the range of Dot's hooves to keep all the milk safely in the bucket. I covered it with a clean linen so I wouldn't have to pick out pieces of hay and dirt when I got it back to the kitchen.

"I have something for you, Lydia."

Oliver was standing by the door silently watching me. He reached into his pocket and took out a shiny red apple. "It's tasty. They grow on my Papa's tree just outside the kitchen door."

I took it in both of my hands and held it to my nose to breathe in the sweet scent. I looked up at him and slowly smiled my approval.

"Thanks, Ollie."

His face changed then. The creases on his forehead disappeared and his light blue eyes lit up as the corners of his mouth lifted.

Thus began the routine of him finding me at the end of the day to give me little things—mostly things he'd find. He said if he thought I'd like it, he'd pick it up and put it in his pocket for me. The next time it was a red hair ribbon with scalloped edges he'd found on the roadside. My collection grew to include more ribbons and buttons, a piece of chalk, a marble, wildflowers, and lady bugs.

I liked that he thought of me. I liked that he gave me tokens of what I came to realize was his affection for me. I showed him appreciation with a smile, and then with a quick kiss on the cheek. Soon, we were holding hands when no one could see us, and in time, we dared our first embrace in the shadows of the barn.

That was the day Pa quit working early. Oliver was at the barn before me, taking care of Blue. The weather was cold enough that we'd already seen our first snow in September. He was certain that 1881 would be another hard winter like the one we'd had the year before, and that we'd have snow stick before Thanksgiving.

I sneaked into the barn and tossed a stone Oliver's way. It landed near him, and he startled at its thud. He looked at it, and I giggled. He turned to see me standing just inside the barn threshold.

"You!" he looked stern, but his eyes were merry as he left Blue to stride over to me.

He wasn't that much taller than me, but he bent over me ominously, and I pushed him away and started to run into the barn. Oliver grabbed my hand and stopped me in my tracks. I pulled against his hand, but not enough to break away.

"Where are you running to, Lydia?" Oliver's voice was low and deep, but not menacing. It was gentle and mesmerizing, and I wanted to melt into it.

I stopped pulling away from his grip, and I started pulling him closer to me until our bodies were touching and I could feel his warm breath on my forehead. I took his other hand and stepped backwards until the sunlight couldn't reach us. My foot caught on something, and I started to fall backwards, but Oliver's grip on my hands tightened, stopping my fall.

"Are you OK, Lydia?"

"Yes, Ollie." I smiled and looked at him from under my eyelashes, "I guess you are strong enough to keep me from falling."

I released my grip from his hands and ran my fingers up his arms to his shoulders. I could feel the muscles underneath his work shirt, and they seemed to tense even more as I ran my hands back down the backs of his arms. His hands wrapped around me and pulled me close to him.

Oliver's heart was beating so hard I could hear it before he pulled away. After just a moment, he stepped away from me and into Blue's stall and started vigorously brushing the tall horse.

I stepped into the stall behind him and softly touched his back.

"I liked that, Ollie. It felt good to have your arms around me."

He froze and said, "It did?"

"Yes. Can we do that again?"

"Maybe another time, Lydia. I'd better go home now," and he set the brush down and ran out of the barn. Oliver jumped on his horse that he pastured in the front while he worked, and kicked it into a gallop as he rode bareback down the road toward his father's farm.

We did do that again, and those brief interludes with Oliver came to be the bright spot in my routine that I'd look forward to all day. My days were full of work—work with Mama in the garden weeding and harvesting; with Pa in the field, seeding and fertilizing; or with the younger ones, helping them study their lessons or making things, especially for birthday or Christmas gifts. In the house, I helped with the cooking, the cleaning, and the ironing. Up before the sun, and to bed after the supper dishes were all done.

Then the long winter was upon us. It wasn't as bad as the year before, but it was still cold and dark, and it made us all long for the warmth of summer. Especially long were the days and weeks when there was no reason for Oliver to come since there was no work to be done, or the snow was too high for anyone to come by for a visit. There was the occasional break in the weather when a brave or restless neighbor would venture out to come calling and break up the monotony. I spent those cold days remembering Oliver's warm embraces and eagerly anticipating more in the coming spring.

Winter eventually wore itself out and gave way to the sunshine. After I finished with my chores, it seemed like Oliver was always nearby to take me for a ride. It felt so good to get out of the house after months of being snowbound inside. We'd bundle up and go riding astride his horse for as long as the sun shared its light with us. We enjoyed taking picnics to eat by the banks of the rivers, and as we passed through the county's many covered bridges, we'd sing or hoot like owls, laughing to hear the sounds we made echo around us. Sometimes we'd make no noise. We'd just stop and listen to the water rush below us, or to the cows lowing outside, or to the wind blowing by, or to the birds in the trees. Oliver and I chased each other down to the river and splashed each other, giggling at the shock of the chilly water on our skin. When we reached home again, we'd run into the dark corners of the barn where we could kiss out of sight of my nosy little brother and sisters, or my busy father who always seemed to have some chore to do outside.

As things heated up between Oliver and I, the world thawed out and spring ushered in the promise of new life.

Ours was a hard-working family, and that was a value we recognized and appreciated in our neighbors. Mama and Pa respected Oliver's father, Peter Franklin, because he was a hard worker, too.

He had emigrated from Germany as a boy. His parents' deaths left him an orphan at a time when young men were expected to enlist in the military. That was not a path he desired to take, so his older sister helped him secure passage to America, and in late spring 1846, 16-year-old Peter boarded the sturdy, three-masted sailing vessel, George Henry, bound for America.

He arrived in early June. He left bustling New York and made his way to Illinois, where he built his reputation as an honest laborer. It was there he met and became enchanted by Rachel Collier, the girl who would become the mother of his children. They married when he was 21 and she was 18.

Mr. Franklin was a young man then, but he had been independent for some years, and he proved he could provide for a family. He established himself as a reliable teamster, hauling loads or pulling heavy farm equipment over fields. Their family grew, and after a decade in Illinois, when he had saved enough money to buy his own team of big strong work horses, he and Mrs. Franklin took their children back and forth across the Midwest, from Wisconsin to Indiana to Missouri, and finally to Iowa. Mr. Franklin had heard among his contacts that Iowa was a good place to raise a family, so he settled down there to farm.

During slow seasons, he'd still harness up the team and go on runs for people. The thriving commerce and construction of their growing community kept Mr. Franklin busy and he often had his sons, Oliver and Fred, help him.

Our families, the Franklins and the Blightons, didn't live next door to each other, but close enough so that one could hop on a horse and be at each other's farm lickety-split. In spite of the demands on our respective farms, our families took advantage of holidays and rare summer Sunday cookouts to gather at our farm or at their farm after church.

The men brought two tables out from the house, placed them under the wide, shady trees, and laid boards on them to make a long table. We had to eat in shifts, since the tables could only seat so many. The oldest of us ate before the youngest, who had to wait their turn. The first ones to eat generally had more sensitive stomachs, so they had time to digest their meal before bedtime later in the evening.

The younger ones were usually so distracted by each other and their fun and games that they took no notice of their hunger pangs anyway. Cranky children and babies were tended to as their mothers saw fit. A cracker here, a grape or two there was just enough to hold them over, but not too much that their appetite was spoiled.

Oliver's and my older siblings had lots of children, for the most part, and we all started our families young. My older sisters and I were all married with babies by the time we were sixteen or seventeen.

My eldest sister, Clary, was the first to leave our parents' home. She married Bill Hendricks when she was sixteen. It was a few years later that Cynthia married Tom Mobley when she was sixteen. Pa always said his second born daughter looked like his mother whose parents were both of Dutch derivation. So we just always called her "Dutch".

A couple of years later, our fifteen-year-old Amy, who Pa named after his mother, married her Ol Stanley. That was just after our older brother Hi, short for Hiram for Pa's father, and my Oliver's older sister, Dora Franklin, married each other the previous summer.

As they all married, our gatherings grew larger, especially when the children started arriving. Holding babies was the only good excuse I could make for not helping the women put all the food out on the table.

Everyone brought something to add to the spread, and we could always count on Clary's specialty: noodles and cabbage boiled in a beef broth. The other usual dishes included fried or roasted chicken, dried beef, cheese, potato salad, apple salad, canned pineapple salad, baked apples, canned pork and beans, corn, canned salmon, several kinds of pickles and jellies, and a variety of cakes. Mama usually baked a couple of pies. We nibbled at olives and pickles while we waited to savor the delicious flavors the table's aromas promised.

"You said it was for keeps!" the boys argued over a game of marbles on a cleared patch of earth.

"No I didn't. I said it was for fair! Why would I say it was for keeps if you didn't bring your marbles with you?"

"But Fred has his."

"Yes, but Fred didn't say it was for keeps either."

"We're playing for fair today. We want to keep our marbles. Next time, bring your marbles and if you have any good ones, we'll play for keeps!"

"OK, I will!"

The children's bare feet padded the ground, kicking up dust as they ran rolling hoops around the yard. Their laughter rang out even though they were out of breath.

If there were newborn animals, we would show them off to the other children. Calves were cute, but I thought they were a bit dumb and smelly, so I preferred to look at the sweet-faced lambs. My favorites to watch were the baby goats that ran around head-butting each other and launching off their mothers' backs. The chicks were the softest to hold and the easiest to reach. The kittens were tricky because the mama cats moved them around if we found them too often.

Sometimes the boys would find a snake or a frog and chase the scaredy-cats around with it. I stayed where I was and pretended to not be a scaredy-cat so they wouldn't bother me. It usually worked.

There was always at least one woman who brought a quilt to work on, and while the women gathered around the frame under a shady tree to add their stitches, they shared their news with each other. My mama, Chloe Gold, was known in Winterset for her finely-stitched hand-made quilts. Family members made sure she knew they wanted one made special for them. She would send away to Sears and Roebucks for scrap bags. Ninety-nine cents could get her some decent sized fabric pieces.

Mama loved to tell how she once made a dress from a nice bit of material she'd received in the mail, "Imagine that. Quilting scraps *and* a dress for ninety-nine cents!"

Pa, Mr. Franklin, and the other men would play horseshoes. The regular clanking of metal on metal, or the heavy thud of metal on sawdust, was punctuated by cheers, or by groans and laughter. Once the older men had their fill of the game, they let the boys take over the pit and settled down to talk about the weather and their crops or whatever work they were doing at the time.

Sometimes they would get into politics, and that inevitably led to someone asking Dutch's husband Tom about the War Between the States. He was a pensive, quiet man, but when he spoke, people listened, for he had an air of authority about him that demanded respect. He also lit up and became animated when he talked of that time in his life.

Tom was older than Dutch by some years, and aside from Mr. Franklin, was the only man present of an age to have fought in the Civil War, for the others were either too old or too young.

Mr. Franklin always said, "I signed up for the draft, but I had a family to support, so President Lincoln never asked me to go to fight."

Tom had been just a boy, and an orphan, when he enlisted in the Union Army.

"I joined up in Springfield, the hometown of Abraham Lincoln!" he'd remind us with evident pride.

The older folks present who could remember the president and the story of his bloody assassination shook their heads from side to side, tsk tsking that his life was cut down too soon by "that actor," they'd call him.

One of the younger children sat on her father's lap, and she asked him, "Who, Papa? Who killed Mr. Lincoln?"

He didn't have a chance to respond before Mama said very resolutely, "We never want to glorify his name by saying it out loud in polite company."

I would take the pitcher of apple cider out to refill glasses when I heard the conversation turn in that direction, for I liked listening to my brother-in-law's stories about "The Great Atlanta Campaign", as he called it, and "General Sherman's March the Sea," although he would often gripe, "It was us foot soldiers doing the marchin'. General Sherman got to ride his horse to the sea."

Nevertheless, I wanted to experience the journey and his adventures through his memories.

"We marched long days, in all kinds of weather, through the states. Occasionally, we'd fight the rebels along the way, but mostly it was just marching at a fast clip. Oh how my muscles ached at night, and my feet had blisters that had blisters on their blisters. We finally got to Atlanta."

Tom never really talked about skirmishes that he was in personally, but he told stories about the men in his company and what he saw happen to them, but not in too much detail, "lest it upset the ladies," he'd always add, looking to Mama, who just nodded her approval.

One story that Tom loved to tell was of a man named John Wilson, who was in another company in his regiment.

"They called him Buck," he began. "Although he was a bit portly, this fellow loved to run everywhere. His unit advanced on the enemy in a double-quick time march through a field of high grass to take the rebel works. They couldn't see the enemy, and so they didn't know what they were running into, and maybe some held back a little because of it. But Buck didn't care. He ran so fast that he was the first to reach the dug-out pit where about 20 rebels lay hiding."

Tom chuckled as he continued, "They say Buck thought fast and pointed his musket at them, yelling 'fight or run, and that damned quick.' And wouldn't you know it, they all surrendered to him!"

The men always laughed with him then, and Mama and Dutch always shook their heads at his use of profanity, especially if children were within earshot.

"Careful, Tom," Dutch warned.

"All but one! The officer!" he continued, his enthusiasm undiminished by his wife's attempt to rein him in. "That man turned and ran!"

Everyone laughed even harder just imagining the scene.

When a child or someone who had never heard him tell the story before was present, it might occur to them to ask Tom what happened to that officer, but Tom never answered. He just shook his head and put his finger to his lips. Winking at whoever asked the question, he finished his story, "Do you know that ole Buck, well he made out pretty good. General Logan made sure he kept that officer's sword."

After dinner, the boys brought watermelons up from the river where they'd been chilling in the cool of the water. We stood to eat the crisp, moist fruit, wiping our chins with our hands so the juice wouldn't run down to our clothes.

Great seed spitting contests were usually initiated by one of the papas, much to the feigned annoyance of the mamas. There were inevitably races and games of strength and endurance masterminded by the young men, and as the hours passed, everyone was plum worn out, especially the children.

By the end of the day, I'd find myself doing the dishes with my younger sister, Minnie, while my older sisters Clary, Dutch, and Amy packed up their leftovers and gathered their children to head out before the lengthening shadows turned the land too dark to drive home.

"Love you," they called out as the horses pulled their wagons away.

"More than tongue can tell," Mama and Pa called back to them, waving goodbye until they reached the end of the drive and turned onto the road.

"She was a bird. She was light. She was grace, wit, and beauty. She was smart in all the ways that matter. She was educated to the eighth grade, so grammar mattered to her. But that was only one way that she shined. She also knew people."

Mr. Franklin eulogized his wife at her unexpected funeral. He wanted mourners to know and appreciate her the way he did.

They did know her. She was the kind of person that people know. Mrs. Franklin was not secretive or reserved. She said what was on her mind, but in a kind way if her opinions differed from others'.

When she gave praise, you knew it was sincere. She had no patience for falsities or niceties that weren't deserved.

As the community filed out of the church, they stopped to offer words of condolence. I was standing close enough to be able to hear them.

"I'm so sorry for your loss, Peter. Rachel sure was a good woman." Mr. Franklin nodded.

"We're sure gonna miss her, Mr. Franklin. She was a gem." He nodded again.

"Keep those happy memories close in your heart, son. She'll stay with you." The two widowers shook hands in mutual understanding.

"I can only try to make apple pie as good as Rachel did, Peter. I wish I'd had her teach me her secrets. When I figure it out, I'll bring one by for you." He dabbed his wet face with a wrinkled handkerchief he pulled out of his pocket.

"Peter, Rachel understood people in a way no one could figure out, like when a dog can sense if you are good or bad. Do you remember when that charlatan came to town and she sniffed him out right away?

She gave him his walking orders in such a way that even he couldn't be mad at her." Mr. Franklin laughed at the memory.

"She had a sense about who people were in their heart," he answered.

I knew myself that she also understood exactly what people needed in order to feel loved. She had a knack for saying just the right thing at the right time, or when words didn't come, a look, or a touch from her could make it all feel right.

It was not long before she passed away, when at one of our family gatherings, someone's wagon rolled over a kitten who was dashing out of the barn and right under the wheels as they came to a stop. The kitten screamed a horrible wail, and when I ran over to it, I realized it was my favorite from Flossie's litter. It was the only one who would let me cuddle it close to my face for any length of time. It rubbed its little cheeks against my nose and then it would scramble down my clothes, usually piercing through the fabric and catching my skin with its razor-sharp claws.

When I reached for the kitten, I realized that the weight of the wagon had crushed its bones and flattened it. His mouth was still open from his cry, and his eyes were open, but I could see there was no life in them anymore. I backed away from him, screaming. As I turned to run away, I crashed into Mrs. Franklin, who just took me in her arms and held me as I sobbed, stroking my head and mumbling comfort into my ear.

She was a mother who didn't discern between her own children and those of us who were not. She nurtured all children, including grown people who still had child-like needs.

My Oliver was ten in 1873 when his mother Rachel died. She had just turned 40, but she seemed healthy. Her death came as a shock to us all.

Mr. Franklin mourned, but he kept his optimistic outlook on life. His sense of humor and personable ways still shined through, but his first love had taken his heart.

Although I was only seven years old when she left this world for the next early that summer, I realized how blessed I was to have known her.

Like everyone in the community, I mourned with her family when she passed away. None had ever known the likes of Rachel Collier Franklin, nor would they again. She was good through and through.

One day, Clary, Dutch, and Amy all came for a visit. Dutch was the one to notice that I was bigger than I had been the last time she visited the month before.

The three of them and Mama were sitting around the kitchen table with their cool apple cider, sharing stories about the neighbors, when Dutch looked at me over the edge of her glass and asked, "How are you, Lydia?"

Her tone was a little sharp, and I feared she was on to me and knew my secret. I continued calmly washing the glass jars in the warm water. I answered in a casual tone, "Fine, Dutch. Keeping busy with the canning and baking."

The other girls also heard the tone in her question. They looked from me to Cynthia, and then back to me. I saw their eyes taking in my form and looking quickly to one another for confirmation of what they each realized.

"Oh yes!" Mama said, "Lydia has put up all the apricots just this morning. You'll each have to take a few jars home to Tom, Bill, and Ol."

Mama saw me every day and took no notice of the subtle changes my body had been going through. She didn't see, or maybe she just didn't want to see, what my sisters' eyes saw very clearly: that not long after I turned sixteen, I'd be a mama, too. They didn't say anything about it. They didn't have to. My sisters' attention to my condition alerted my mama, whose eyes took in my changed body with a fresh perspective. Then they rested on my face. I had to look away from her.

When the girls left to go home, she grabbed my wrist as we stood on the porch waving goodbye to them.

"Is it true, Lydia? Have you gotten yourself in the family way?"

I couldn't speak, and I tried to bring my sisters back with the force of my will, by the intensity of my gaze.

"Look at me, Lydia. Answer your mother."

I had been so afraid of this moment. Mama's voice was stern, but when I looked at her, there was only concern in her eyes. When I did not bleed for a couple of months, I thought I might have lost track of time, but when a third month passed, I became terrified of what was happening in my body, but I couldn't talk to anyone about it, even Oliver. Especially Oliver.

He and I had done things we knew we weren't supposed to be doing, but he had told me that if I jumped around afterward, it should be fine. I felt silly doing it, but I jumped around quite a bit in the days after.

Mama's grip tightened on my wrist and her eyebrows rose. She did not have to repeat her question. I simply nodded, and she exhaled and shook her head.

"Oh, my dear child, now you've done it. What are we to do now? Shame on you, Lydia. Whatever will your father say? Oh, dear Lord, please forgive us." Mama had let go of me, and she was pacing back and forth, wringing her hands anxiously.

It seemed like her emotions were conflicting—one moment compassionate, the next angry, the next fearful, the next contrite. I had already experienced all these feelings and more, so I watched her to see where she would land. I never wanted to disappoint her or cause her or Pa to feel ashamed of me.

"I'm so sorry, Mama."

"You'll be sorry when your Pa finds out."

"Oh, Mama, please don't tell him."

Mama stopped her pacing and laughed at me. "Don't tell him? Your body will tell him soon enough. Your crying baby will tell him soon enough." She shook her head and took up her pacing again.

"When he comes in from his work, I'll tell him then. You leave it to me."

I had no choice for I was but a child myself. When Pa came home, Mama took him into their bedroom and closed the door. After her muffled voice stilled, a silence answered that was so thick, I wanted to run away. I was in the kitchen, where Mama had set me down at the table with the potatoes to peel for dinner. My hands held potato and knife, but forgot to do the task and were still. After only a moment, Pa came out of their room quietly and just stood and looked at me.

"Is it true, daughter? Are you in the family way?"

I could only nod at him.

"Oliver?"

I nodded again.

His eyes lowered to the ground, and he breathed out a heavy sigh, but he didn't say another word. Pa put his hat on as he left the kitchen, and he took his wagon down the road in the direction of the Franklin's farm.

The coming arrival of Oliver's child was a surprise to our parents, and they were none too pleased, but what were they going to do? Oliver was only seventeen, so Mama and Pa, and Mr. Franklin agreed that I'd stay home with the baby while Oliver worked in Winterset at the feed and seed store. He would save up enough money to marry me in a couple of years and be able to take care of us.

That is how it happened. For nearly two years, they made sure we kept our distance from one another. But any time Oliver could sneak away, he'd come and let me know he was there by chucking little pebbles at my window, just hard enough to make a sound, but not hard enough to break the glass. I brought little James out with me so we wouldn't end up doing again what made that baby in the first place.

I was never so happy as the day Oliver married me because then no one could talk about me at the Grange or at the mercantile anymore. It even silenced them at the church. I was finally made an honest woman, and oh how grateful I was. It was like a fresh slate wiped clean and shiny new.

Even though what I learned at church was that being intimate before marriage made one dirty, I didn't feel dirty. I didn't have any reservations about letting Oliver love me because he was so sincere, and he did think of me and care for me, as I cared for him.

My mama didn't seem to understand how I could let that happen to me when she had raised me in the church. I knew the rest of the world also saw me as a sinner, but I kept my head up. What was done was done, no turning back.

I didn't want to turn back anyway. I loved nothing more than my little boy, and Oliver was kind to me. He was going to be the kind of man I could devote my life to. He made me feel good when we were together. He made my knees weak when he put his hand on the small of my back, and I felt safe when I was with him. Oliver was as capable with a plow as he was with charming me, so I knew he'd be able to provide for me and our son.

Oliver surprised us all when he announced, just after our marriage ceremony at Pa's house that he was taking me and the baby to Nebraska in the days to come.

"There is good land to be had for growing crops out there, and I figure it is time to go out and make my way in the world, farming the land."

Mama's fork clattered against her plate as it fell from her fingers. She didn't say anything, but looked to Pa, and then to me. Her gaze held mine for a moment, but there were no tears in her eyes like there were in mine. I realized that I was Oliver's now, and there was nothing she or I could say about it. It was as much news to me as it was to them.

Pa nodded his head as he chewed his apricot cobbler and said, "I'd heard there's good land to be had out Nebraska way. Good for growing corn!" He didn't look at me.

As the men talked soil and seed, I took little James on my lap and held him close until he squirmed away, eager to chase the kitten running through the kitchen. I picked up my fork but couldn't eat another bite of cobbler.

What was I going to do without Mama and Pa? I'd be too far away for Dutch or Amy or Clary to come visit me often. My mind was racing, and my heart was beating so fast I could hear it in my ears. I'd never been anywhere but in Iowa. How would I manage on a distant farm alone with a baby?

Lots of people had tried their hand at homesteading in Nebraska only to fail or give up. This left plenty of opportunities to pick up good land at a low cost. We all moved to Nebraska in the spring of 1885. My father-in-law convinced four of his adult children to go with him to claim some of this land.

Arvilla was his eldest daughter. She and her husband were well-settled in Iowa and didn't feel the need to move their family west. I wished we could be as rooted there.

Fred, Oliver's older brother, was 28. He brought his reluctant wife, Youtha, and their two children, John and Bertha. He came to help his father and Oliver break the sod for our new homes in Nebraska.

Dora, who was married to my brother, Hi, was 26 and had also come with their little girl, Myrtle. They were eager to explore new possibilities for their family in Nebraska.

Mary was 24, and because she was unmarried and still lived with their father, she was obliged to leave her sister and her friends behind in Iowa and move with him.

My new husband felt that his best chance at making a life for me and our baby was to try his hand at farming the western prairie, so of course we went along with all of them.

When Mr. Franklin decided to take his family west, Susan, his second wife of nearly "ten long years" as he often said, refused to go. Mr. Franklin was matter of fact and determined. He would not be held back, nor would he have his life be limited. He divorced her and left her in Iowa.

Arvilla would report in her letters that the community was shocked by his poor treatment of her. Eventually, my sister-in-law wrote that her former step-mother landed on her feet, for it wasn't even two years later that the former Mrs. Franklin married another man, 21 years her junior.

"He can have her!" said Mr. Franklin when he read the news. "And good luck with that one!"

Oliver's father kept moving on. It's not that he didn't care for Susan, but she was just not Rachel, his first wife and the love of his life who had left him a widower when she was still young and beautiful. He would reminisce about her throughout his life. Although he would marry again, and he loved and enjoyed his other wives, I knew that his heart never truly belonged to anyone like it had belonged to the mother of his children.

I had been married to Oliver a short time when I became aware of the fact that our second baby would be born in Nebraska. I was so busy with preparations for our move, but that stopped me in my tracks. The thought of carrying and delivering a little one without the help of my sisters and the comfort of my mama was overwhelming to me. I was terrified the entire nine months as we packed, prepared, moved and got settled in.

We journeyed by train. Although the trip was not very long, each mile westward across the wide prairies felt like 100 miles. Vast areas of empty, open, uninhabited land were punctuated by a farmhouse every once in a great while. There were lone shanties at the occasional stop, like at our destination, Seward. It was a simple structure with a sign announcing its location, and now ours.

Our meager possessions sat piled around us as the train pulled away toward the barren western horizon. I had been unmoored from my family, but the further away we rode, I was surprised to realize that our journey would not be long enough for me. I wished I were still on the train. I feared I would never go any further.

Strangers pointed us in the direction we wanted to go. There was a general store and a hotel up the road a bit. We stayed there until Mr. Franklin secured the homestead.

Oliver was 22, I was nineteen, and our son was three when we settled with my new family on our new land. The men saw to clearing and breaking up the land and then they sowed it to corn. I tended to my little James and helped my sister-in-laws make the temporary sod house habitable for all of us until Fred and Youtha, and Dora and Hi, left with their families to start their own farms. Then it was just the five of us. Mary and I started a garden that would provide plenty of fresh vegetables for our table.

Even though Oliver's older sister was with us, I felt so alone and lonely when our brothers and sisters left us to move to their own farms. Mary was the only person I talked to all day long, and what we talked about was no different from day to day. I was busy from before the sun rose until long after the sun slipped below the horizon, so there was no time to go visiting anyway. We had neighbors a few miles away in each direction, but only a few ladies, who no doubt were busy with their own farms.

Oliver and Mr. Franklin came in for meals, but were so bone tired, they barely spoke to each other, let alone to us women, and when they did converse, it was often in German. Although they used many English words in their conversation, I couldn't always follow what they were saying. Oliver would tell me it was about the wood frame house they were building for us, or their crops and farming; things that didn't concern me and would just bore me. I had nothing to contribute even if I could understand them.

James could speak a bit, but he wasn't yet forming complete sentences, so talking with him was useless. He seemed to prefer the words "why?" and "no!" which didn't exactly lend themselves to civil conversation.

When my father-in-law spoke in his heavily accented English, I enjoyed hearing about his travels. As he occasionally rummaged about in his memories, I hung on Mr. Franklin's every word, allowing myself to be carried off through his remembrances of places I would never see, like distant Bremen in Germany, and cosmopolitan New York. He described many people he'd met, like the man who had tried to steal his money as he got off the ship, and honest people, like my father, who helped steer him along the right path in settling into his new country. He described decisions he had made, such as when he left his fatherland to avoid conscription in a military he didn't want to fight in and give his life for and came to America as a young man.

Oliver usually changed the subject, perhaps because he'd heard it all before. Maybe because he himself had no desire to venture forth into the larger world. He had told me as much. I would have loved to have seen Bremen and New York with my own eyes, but I knew I never would. My world was only going to be as big as Oliver's.

We hadn't been in Nebraska long before Mr. Franklin met Widow Perkins. Soon after that he married her, as she was certain in her expectations of how a man and a woman should relate properly to one another. She would not tolerate a mere hint of impropriety.

She called her new husband "Mr. Franklin" even in the privacy of their own home that they shared with her three youngest children, 15-year-old boy and girl twins, Emil and Nellie, and a 10-year-old boy named Jimmy.

Although he insisted on calling her "Mrs. Perkins" even after they were married, Mr. Franklin was not nearly as formal with her. He enjoyed scandalizing his new wife by swatting her on the backside as she walked by him. She always protested, but her eyes shone as she turned away from those of us in the room, struggling to suppress a smile. It looked to me like she took a bit of secret delight in his playfulness.

As my belly grew larger and larger, memories of my first pregnancy, and labor, came back vividly. These were memories I had not allowed myself to think about because of my shame. Now my experience was not of shame, it was a kind of pride in having proved myself a good, fruitful wife. Yet, I also felt fear.

There was a doctor in town, but he could be a good two hours away. I had no experienced womenfolk to help me through the pregnancy, and more importantly, through the labor. Mary had never experienced it, and she was so squeamish, she had refused to help when her own sister delivered her baby. Would Oliver have to deliver our child? I cringed at the thought of that.

Thankfully, word of my condition got around the community and the neighbor ladies paid me a visit one day. The kind women reassured me that when the time came, I'd just need to send the men to get them and they'd come right away to help me deliver my baby. And that is how it happened on a cold November day. We named her Jessie Edith.

It wasn't even a year later when our precious baby girl left us. Oliver buried her under an old, gnarled tree about 800 feet behind the house. I went out and stood by the little grave wearing my black shawl over the brown calico dress I'd had on for the three days baby Jessie was ailing. She burned with fever as I desperately tried to restore her to health.

Mr. Franklin said a brief prayer in heavily accented English, and then a longer one in German that I didn't understand. I watched the brown earth cover my swaddled baby with each shovelful that took her further and further away from me. The rhythmic, heavy thud of the dirt hitting her little wooden coffin confirmed that I would never hold her body in my arms again.

When Oliver patted the mound of earth with the back of the shovel, I turned and walked back to the house. I was numb to the cries of my son as he followed behind me, plucking at my shawl, crying.

"Mama? Mama?! I hungee, Mama."

I barely heard Mary tell him, "Come with me, James. We'll get some breakfast now."

I climbed into my bed, pulled the covers over my head, and allowed merciful sleep to take me away from the cruel heartache I felt, and the excruciating pain in my breasts as they swelled and leaked the wasted milk that wasn't needed anymore.

My second daughter, Bessie, arrived and brightened our farm in the middle of that winter. She was a pretty and plump little thing that smiled early, although she could get feisty quick when anyone told her no. She took our minds off our losses and helped us count our blessings. Bessie's blue eyes lit up especially when her big brother paid her any attention, or when he came bursting into the house from playing outside.

It was that winter when the big Christian revival came to our small community in Goehner a little ways south of Seward. Mama and Pa had decided to move to Nebraska with my sister Amy and her family when they joined us the year after we came west.

Mama had been religious since she was a girl and always encouraged us all to find comfort in reading the Bible. She wanted us to get right with the Lord before it was too late. I know it weighed heavy on Mama's mind that she may have to be in heaven with Jesus for all eternity without the pleasure of Pa's company, for he never made any declaration of his beliefs; that is, until that winter.

I had just had the baby, so I stayed home from the revival. When Amy came for a visit later that week, she described to me how she and her husband, Ol, and even my Oliver, but especially when our Pa all got up and walked down the aisle to accept Jesus as their savior when the young, blind preacher invited new believers to come to the altar. How thrilled our Mama was.

"I've never seen anything like it, Lydia. When we came back to our seats from the altar, Mama's face was wet with tears of joy. Her hands were raised to the ceiling, and she laughed out loud. She embraced each of us in turn and shouted 'Hallelujah!' to the heavens. I wish you'd been there to see it, sister."

I wished I'd seen it with my own eyes as well. Our mother was not one to show her emotions in such an animated manner. She made her pleasure or displeasure known in more subtle ways like a simple smile, or a pat on the cheek, or a frown. She would pace the floor and wring her hands and make brief statements of anger or disappointment. I'd felt the sting of her slap once, maybe twice, when I was defiant as a child, but she never raised her voice in anger to any of us.

At the same time, I was relieved that I had not been there to feel the pressure to leave my seat and walk up to the altar in front of the congregation. Like my mother, I was not one to share my deep feelings with anyone, particularly not when it came to my faith. I had not yet made my mind up about my faith anyway, so to take the walk up the aisle would have been dishonest, yet to not take the walk would have been a disappointment for my mother.

I wondered if that's why my husband did it, or why Pa did it. But then Pa laid the foundation for the new church in Goehner, so he must have been devoted on some personal level. It would be another eight years before I devoted my life to Christ and became a member of the Methodist Church in Seward in an effort to keep wholesome thoughts in my mind and stay a loyal wife.

Mansel Gold was Mama's father. It was a solid-sounding name, and his son, my Uncle Hi, short for Hiram Mansel, was named for him. We named our fourth child Ernest Mansel to keep the name going in the family.

I had just given birth to Ernest on June 11, 1888, when after only a year and five months of life and a couple days of illness, Bessie left us suddenly in the middle of the hot summer.

Somehow understanding the solemnity of the moment, my five-year-old James was quiet and still for once. He stood against the wall in the kitchen, just watching while I wiped down Bessie's body for the last time and wrapped it snuggly in her softest blanket.

Oliver and I buried Bessie alone. He dug the grave next to her sister's on the edge of our property and gently placed Bessie's little wooden coffin at the bottom of it. Oliver said a prayer and shoveled the dirt back into the hole he had made. I laid the fistful of wildflowers I picked atop the fresh mound.

And so, I suffered the loss of two babes after Oliver and I married and moved to Nebraska. The shock that followed the joy of anticipation was nearly more than I could bear... twice.

I wanted each of those baby girls so much. Perhaps they were my chance at redemption. I needed to free myself of the shame I felt from having my older boy, James, out of time and order.

Don't get me wrong; I wanted James, too, once he had been born and I fell in love with him. I just didn't like it when people were very interested in him when he was a baby. I might have to tell them I was an unmarried mother, and they'd think I was a sullied girl. I didn't have to worry about that anymore. I was a married woman now and my reputation was no longer in danger. And now I had two sons.

Because my second son was only a month old when our Bessie passed away, I had to care for him regardless of how devastated I was. My father-in-law and my sister-in-law had both married and left the farm soon after Bessie was born, so I couldn't ignore Ernest and count on someone else to care for him when he cried out in hunger or when he needed his diaper changed, as they'd done for James when baby Jessie left us.

James turned 6 that winter, but he was too young to be unsupervised for long, and too small to be of any help on the farm, but Oliver took him along to work in the barn or in the fields after the spring thaw to relieve me. He must have managed just fine because our oldest son returned to me in one piece each day.

Baby Ernest slept when he wasn't eating, and I slept when he slept, which was a lot at first. That meant I neglected my housework, but Oliver was kind and understanding until I could rouse myself to take care of him and our boys.

That fall, Oliver had a chance to go with a threshing machine from farm to farm to help with the harvesting. Because Ernest was so new, Oliver didn't want me to stay alone, so he rode out six or seven miles on old Dock to get my little sister, Grace, who was nine, to come and stay with me. She and our parents were staying close to Amy and her family in Hastings since they all moved to Nebraska the year after we left Iowa.

As they galloped up to the house, I could see that Oliver had a bundle of Grace's clothes in front of him, and she sat behind him. The wind had loosed wisps of red hair from her braids, and her deep-set blue eyes, which reminded me of our Pa's, sparked in her flushed, round face.

"I was hanging on for dear life, for he didn't go slow!" she exclaimed as I reached up to help her off the tall horse.

"You did just fine," Oliver reassured her as he walked Dock past us and out to the pasture. He still had to prepare to leave early in the morning for a job that would bring us good money. He thought it was worth it to leave me alone for weeks with our newborn son, too soon after the death of our second little girl.

I was so grateful to have my younger sister Grace's company. We took the wagon for an excursion into town one day. After we ate our picnic lunch on the lawn in the courthouse square and threw a ball with James, we went into the mercantile where I got some calico. When we got home, I made Grace a new dress. Our mother had taught us all to sew by hand. I let my little sister help and she sewed the straight seams using my new sewing machine for the first time.

Grace helped me care for the baby and she entertained James. She also did other little things like set the table for meals and help me with the dishes. The thing I appreciated her help with the most was digging the potatoes, for it was difficult for me to crouch low and get on my knees since I was still recovering from having Ernest. She didn't like it much, complaining the dirt got stuck under her fingernails, but she did it.

Aside from all the chores she did for me, I treasured our special time together when it was just us, so I could get to know my younger sister better. I was already twelve by the time she was born, so we were not especially close the way I was with our older sisters. It cheered me to be with her and just talk.

After the boys were asleep and the dishes were done one evening, we were sitting at the kitchen table when Grace told me about her close call with death. A winter tornado ripped the roof right off our older sister Amy's house one night, just hours before Amy gave birth to her fifth child, Elmer Thomas.

"I had been staying with Amy because she was sick. Her husband, Ol, had gone after Mother when Amy called for her, and when he was gone, a terrible wind came up. I guess it was a tornado. We were scared almost to death, and I was hoping and praying that it would soon stop, but it grew worse, and the windows began to fall in."

"The windows fell in?" I asked, incredulous.

Grace nodded. "Amy grabbed a quilt off the bed and wrapped it around herself and told me to get the children and come on. We got to the door and the roof went off over our heads and the wall caved in on the beds where the children had been laying a few moments before."

"What?" I couldn't believe my ears. I'd heard Amy's house was destroyed in a storm, but I hadn't yet heard the details.

"It was so dark we couldn't see a thing except when the lightning would flash, but we managed to get to the home of Frank Scranton about a quarter of a mile away. His house hadn't been damaged at all. He insisted on Amy lying down on his bed, and he hung his lantern in the window for a sort of beacon light."

"Oh, thank goodness for the neighbor! Where were Mama and Pa? And Ol?" I asked.

"They came as soon as the storm subsided. Pa and Mama brought another neighbor and his wife. They expected to find some of us killed. They got us all in a wagon and took us home to our place and we children had to go to the neighbors'. The next day, there was another baby boy."

Little did she know, six years after that baby was born, my sister Grace would go on to marry that kind neighbor Frank Scranton and have nine babies of her own.

As we talked, we found we had common memories of growing up, despite our difference in age. She reminded me of waking up very early in the morning hearing Pa hewing out ax handles.

"Remember?" she asked. "Pa had a special room for hewing, and he made lots of handles for sale. Remember how people used to say he made extra good ax handles?"

I did remember, and it was comforting to me. She had other memories which were not as comforting.

"How about that time we were down by the creek and Mama and the girls were doing the laundry. Remember when I ran by that old log, and I stepped on a big brown snake before I saw it lying there? I wasn't wearing any shoes! Do you remember? I was in hysterics! I have shivers just thinking on it, Sis!"

I also had shivers, but her recollections of playing down by the water while Mama was doing the laundry, heating the water in a big iron kettle there, took me right back to Iowa. I missed the soft rolling green hills and shady rivers.

There were trees and hills and rivers in Nebraska, but somehow it was a land with an edge. The landscape was harder. It could be stark and empty, and the wind was more insistent in Nebraska. Young trees were planted in rows of windbreaks along property lines to give relief from the harsh weather that could blow from the north. The weather still came, though.

Grace helped me see our new home state with a more appreciative eye.

"Lydia, when we came with Amy and Ol in those covered wagons—oh my, what a thrill to see that first windmill! I'd never see one before, Lydia."

"Well, Mr. Franklin brought us out on the train, but the windmills were one of the first things I had noticed as well."

She looked up at me then and gave me a big grin.

We sat by the open kitchen door where the light was bright and direct, stitching pieces of her new dress by hand. We used short, even stitches, the way Mama taught us. It would be fresh and bright and crisp for a time, until wear had loosened the seams a bit and the fabric had conformed to the shape of Grace's body.

As we sewed a new garment, my little sister and I pieced together a new relationship with one another. We weren't just older sister and younger sister anymore. We became friends.

Grace also helped me mend some things: old socks with holes in the toes and heels, shirtwaists with missing buttons or raveling seams, dish towels with fraying edges.

As Oliver's and my wardrobes were given new life, my heart felt like it was mending as well. We stitched together the sharp edges of my heart, jagged from the loss of not just one, but two children; and the grief and the guilt and the disappointment, and the fear that it would happen again—that I would lose another child to the Grim Reaper. I could never be seamless, whole, and new like I was when we first came to Nebraska, but I could be functional and productive again.

I had such a hard time getting back to my daily chores when we buried the babies. The memory of my children's sweet faces at my breast and the thought of their precious bodies in the cold ground made me feel unsettled. I paced the floor, especially at night. I wanted to reclaim their bodies and wrap them in fresh blankets and cradle them in my arms. I wanted to see to it that they knew their Mama was still here for them. And then I remembered they didn't need me—they were safe with our Redeemer, as my mama always referred to Him.

That was a relieving thought, until my ire got up at the thought that He should be enjoying the company of my babies after he stole them from me. That didn't seem too loving to me. I questioned the purpose of it all. What was the purpose of my having them, the purpose of their brief little lives, and the purpose of their deaths?

None of it made any sense to me, and the futility of it all angered me. I felt I was being toyed with, made a fool of. A fool for believing that I had been so blessed with each of my little girls, when I only had them for a short while, and then they were taken so soon.

I wondered whether it was my fault. What did I do to make God take them back? Wasn't I a good enough mother? Was I being punished? Did the sins of my childhood weigh on their souls? I hoped not. Oh God, I hoped not. They were innocents. What kind of loving Father would bring so much pain upon His faithful child?

Mama had always told me to, "have faith in God, for he knows you and loves you even better than I do." I had trusted her, and in my deepest heart was a feeling that I would never share aloud with anyone. I resented her. She obviously didn't know God's heart as well as she claimed to. What had she been told? She believed it, and it wasn't true, but she taught those lies to us anyway. Oh Mama.

When I was alone, these thoughts plagued me throughout my waking hours, and I felt perpetual fear, shame, and anger. When Grace came, my mind had other places to go. Oliver had known this, and that is why he insisted she come be with me when he went off to work. How grateful I was to him.

Mama's rheumatoid arthritis eventually flared up and it always slowed her down with horrible pain, so Grace returned home to help her.

That time with my little sister was a rare chance to be together just with each other and relive old happy times together. We never spoke of my babies—I didn't want to make her uncomfortable or start to cry in front of her.

I always noticed how people were afraid to mention my babies once they were buried. Although I thought of them every day and wanted to always keep the memories of them fresh, speaking of the dead, even to loved ones, was just not to be done. They didn't want to remind me of the thing that never left my mind. I didn't want to make them feel I needed anything from them, like the understanding or the comfort they could never possibly provide.

I would never forget. My little girls would always be in my thoughts—nearly every moment of every day. Even after the sharp stabbing pain in my heart that knocked me to my knees at first had dulled to a deep quiet ache; and even after I was finally able to draw a full breath into my lungs, I still lived with the pain and the longing for them, and I knew I would the rest of my days.

I dared not hope to know my fourth baby, Ernest, but as time passed and he thrived, a part of my broken heart rejoined me, and I was able to enjoy his charms.

Two more years. That was all we had to get through until the land was officially ours and the title transferred to our name. Nebraska had been our home for three years already.

Although I was not in solitude, living with my husband and our boys on the farm, my loneliness was unbearable at times. It was an ache and a longing for the familiar companionship that I had taken for granted while living at home with my parents and my sisters and our brothers. We lived in comfortable understanding of one another's patterns and habits and rhythms. I never felt that silences needed to be filled as I did with Oliver's family. I relaxed some when his father and sister moved away.

I did miss having Mary around after she married the bachelor from down the road. The neighbor women were kind, friendly, and generous, but I was never at ease with them. I never took them into my confidence about anything. I had little patience for the gossip and small talk that they loved to share.

I didn't understand how Oliver could be out on the land all day, completely alone with just the horses and not have anything to say to me when he came in for supper. I always had so much to tell him about; usually what the boys had come up with, or what our dog, Shep, had gotten into. But my husband barely grunted anything in response, except sometimes to say "Lydia, you sure do go on about nothin'."

I never told him he hurt my feelings, but I'd get quiet and let James and little Ernest go on to their Papa about nothing. Oliver may not have said much back, but he patiently listened to them, and once he was through eating, he'd take them on his lap or get on the floor with them to play with the top or the wooden blocks he'd made for them until I took our boys away to clean them up and put them to bed.

I sought to ease the empty feeling in me by keeping busy. There was always something to do around the farm or in the house. There was always something to weed or pick, or milk or feed or clean up after, or cook or sew or put away. My daily routine became rote, but when I didn't have to think about what I was doing was when I would most miss my sisters and my mother. They had all moved away, either back to Iowa or to western Nebraska. And Amy went all the way to Montana with her family.

In time, Oliver and I had ten children: five sons and five daughters, and thankfully I was blessed to know seven of them through their childhoods. I was happy to have daughters, but one doesn't interact with daughters as casually as one does with sisters or girlfriends. I didn't anyway.

I always felt that some distance was appropriate and good so my daughters wouldn't miss the lessons they must learn; lessons like how to be a good Christian girl, and a wife and a mother. Because I had three older sisters to help teach me, sometimes I felt like I had four mothers rather than one. I didn't know any different, but they seemed so much closer to Mama than I was. I never felt like I could get as close to her as I wanted, but I figured that was a good distance to keep with my own girls.

Of course I loved my husband and our children, but I yearned for more. I wanted new experiences, new sensations. I know that sounds quite shocking and it's not something I would ever tell just anyone, but it's where Oliver and I were different in our interests.

Oliver rarely spoke to me because I do believe he thought he knew everything there was to know about me, and I came to think that maybe he just didn't care enough to really know me. Yet, I was guilty of the same with him.

He really did think of nothing but seed, fertilizer, weather, and his blasted (forgive me) corn. I knew this because when he did speak to any other adult, that's all he talked about. That and the market, which never provided the prices he'd earned for his hard labor and care through the seasons of planting, weeding, and harvesting. He had a one-track mind, and I often felt I was not on that track.

If I had to really confess something, I'd say I missed the young Ollie that charmed me with gifts of sweet nothings and stolen kisses in the barn shadows. I wondered if he missed the girl I once was, too.

But no. Probably not.

Pa married Mama and they lived near their families in Wisconsin until the West beckoned them. They called five more counties home by the time I was born in Minnesota, joining four elder siblings.

Our parents kept moving from territory to territory, from state to state, eventually landing in Iowa. That is, until Pa decided they should come join the family in Nebraska.

The year after we left for Nebraska, my parents left their oldest daughters, Clary and Dutch, and the grandchildren behind to move closer to us in a shared adventure.

My Pa was born and grew up in the same New York home. When his 45-year-old father longed to go west, Pa went with his parents and all but one of his siblings to Wisconsin.

Like my father, Oliver's father was always restless. Mr. Franklin enjoyed moving and having new experiences, new homes, new endeavors, and new relationships.

Oliver was not like our fathers in the ways that they were adventurous. He didn't mind being rooted in one place and repeatedly doing the same tasks, or even eating the same food every day.

After a long winter's diet of root vegetables and salt pork, Oliver would have been quite content to tolerate it into the spring and summer when berries and fruits of the orchard were available to us aplenty, along with the fresh cruciferous vegetables I grew in the garden. I started with radishes and broccoli, then cabbage and cauliflower, and finally turnips and Brussels sprouts. They all came up magically out of the ground.

On occasion, Oliver managed to snare a rabbit in his trap, but taking the life of a little creature always seemed to make him even more pensive and sober than usual. He wasn't much of a shot with the rifle, but he arranged for our son James to go out hunting with our neighbor Mr. Sloan, who taught him along with his sons Esau and Jesse, how to shoot and dress game.

Our son became a capable hunter, so he would set off to hunt on his own. At first, he practiced on prairie dogs, but eased his way to killing larger game like wild turkeys, grouse, and an occasional deer, which he would take to the Sloan farm to butcher. They would smoke the meat for us and then James would go to get it after about a week or so. He left some of the meat with them as thanks but brought home enough meat to feed our family for some time.

I kept chickens, so we had eggs, and our cow and a few goats gave us milk which we drank and I made butter and cheese with it. Our garden always gave us such an abundance of vegetables and berries that I was happy to can, pickle, and bake enough to share with the neighbors.

When Oliver took me with him into Seward, I would line a big flat-bottomed basket with my favorite red gingham cloth and fill it with jars and pies along with fresh butter to sell at the mercantile.

I always felt lucky to get into town because Oliver was not just satisfied eating the same foods every day, he was also fine with doing the same things day after day. Not that farming is easy, but he did the same types of tasks every day, varying, of course, by the season.

I longed to go into Seward. It wasn't a big town, but the thought of seeing goods we hadn't made, and seeing other people and other horizons beyond our own was thrilling to me. Oliver had little use for towns, and rarely did he find a reason to go, let alone entertain my requests to go with him.

Once I had joined my life with Oliver's, I did what I watched my mother and my sisters and every other woman I knew do and I became someone's wife and a mother. I didn't realize it at the time, but I gave up who I was as an individual. I sacrificed what I wanted and did without what I needed so my husband and children would never go without.

It took me a long time to realize that the sense of discomfort, of anxiety, of restlessness, of longing that I often felt was just evidence of what I had let go of in clinging to another, of whom I had lost: myself, or the chance to get to know myself anyway.

I had worked for years making sure Oliver never regretted taking me on, marrying me when it seemed he could have married any of the prettier girls in the county. I figured he was obligated to marry me because I'd let my curiosity get the better of me, and I carried the growing evidence for nine months. It never would have happened had I kept a penny locked between my knees as Mama always told me to do. I let the penny fall, and it got lost in that hay loft above the stables in Pa's barn, along with my maidenhood.

Oliver was never much on long-winded conversation, but he spoke to me that particular rainy spring afternoon about his dreams and his plans for the future. It was a future that included me. I felt reassured that he saw our future together, and when he described a life and a family we would have as I lay in his strong arms under a warm horse blanket, I could see it, too. I wanted that, and I let him in again. It felt good to be loved and wanted. He kissed me deeply, and we breathed each other in.

Sitting on the edge of my bed on the Mother's Dream quilt of pink and white with blue geometric figures my mama had made for me, I thought back to that sweet afternoon.

In my right hand, I gripped a hairbrush and drew it through the ends of a fistful of hair I held in my left hand, pulling it through the tangles that had woven their way together as I slept.

My long auburn hair had glints of gray flowing throughout its waves. It reached the bottom of my back, and I was able to wind the length of it around my hand to form a bun that I secured with pins at the back of my head. The bun was loose enough that no hairs pulled too tightly. A few wisps that had escaped the confines of the bun framed my face. They tickled my cheeks when the breeze caught it and spun it around as I worked outside feeding the chickens or hanging up the laundry to dry in the sunshine.

Whenever I looked at myself in a mirror, I could see my mother's face. It became more and more like hers with each passing year. Like hers, my mouth was permanently turned down so that even if I was content, my frown tricked others into believing I was cross.

I did not smile enough to have creases at the corners of my eyes. I was not concerned about lines on my face like Dutch was. She was such a beauty as a girl, losing her youth and glow distressed her as she faded with age.

I didn't worry about my facial expressions as I drew the cloth apron around my waist over my work dress. It was a shapeless, loose-fitting garment that was well-suited for working in the garden and bringing the cow into the barn to be milked. The large apron kept the baking flour off the skirt at the same time as it kept the dirt from Oliver's corn fields from getting onto the bread dough as I kneaded it on the wood block table in the kitchen.

I had another work dress, and a dark dress for church, which was a little nicer. My younger sister Gracie had helped me sew it to fit my form better.

Over time, my body had become fleshy all over. I ate well on the farm's bounty, and my body was a public display of that abundance as well as the burdens of childbearing it had endured ten times. My generous thighs rubbed together as I walked, and the friction shredded the legs of my undergarments, so I had to patch and mend them every few months or so.

I cared more about comfort on a daily basis than appearances, so I was glad to live far from public eyes.

My ample, pendulous breasts were not confined in a corset as I worked around the farm. They swung with the momentum of my arm as I scattered the corn on the ground for the hens to peck at. I tucked my shift up under them to catch the sweat that would otherwise collect and drip down my waist.

My pace was quick for carrying the heavy load that was my body, as there was too much to get done in one day to take any time to pause or change direction.

Even when I sat to shell the peas, I perched on the edge of a chair I'd brought outside by the kitchen door. Knees wide apart, toes pointed outward, I bent over a pot, emptying the peas to be boiled on the stove top and chucking the pods to the sides where the clucking chickens waited to pluck them up in their greedy beaks.

That task done, I moved my small feet quickly to get to the pump, where I yanked on the handle rapidly until cool, clear water gushed out and into the bucket that held the cooking and washing-up water for the kitchen. As I put the bucket on the stove, I could smell that the bread baking in the oven was just about as browned on top as I wanted it to be, so I moved to the table to grab the towels that protected my hands as I pulled the loaves out of the hot oven.

That was how my days were spent, running from one task to another.

Late one morning, Oliver was in the fields and the children were at school when I had an unusual visitor. I was enjoying being in the house all by myself, when I was startled by the high-pitched voice calling my name.

"Mrs. Franklin?"

Who on earth could that be? I put the last loaf of bread atop the cooling rack on the stove. Wiping my hands on my apron, I went to the back door and looked through the screen to a man in a top hat. He wore dark leather suspenders over his white shirt, which was stretched taut across his round belly. He hung his thumbs in the loops of his waistband. His boots were worn, but they were cleaner than Oliver's, so I knew this man didn't spend much time in the fields like my husband did. He was standing under our young apple tree, looking toward the house, waiting for my response.

"Who might that be?" I called back from inside, knowing he couldn't see me clearly.

"M' name's Ziglar. I come from the Schultz's down the way. They said you might be needin' some kitchen wares."

I was caught off-guard. I didn't know how to respond, so I didn't. My mind hadn't caught up with the unexpected pause in activity. It was still racing ahead in the order of what I needed to do.

"I sell kitchen wares," he said to break the brief silence. "I sell farming tools, too, if your husband be needin' any of those."

I stepped out from behind the screen door to get a better look at the man and his rig, which had shiny metal objects hanging from the sides. Curly salt and pepper hair hung nearly to his shoulders, and his long beard and shaggy mustache were obviously not tended to regularly. I guessed he didn't have a woman to look after him. I kept Oliver's hair and face as trimmed up when he'd let me.

This Mr. Ziglar didn't smile, but his face was friendly. He continued, "I have baking pans and rolling pins, too."

His dark eyes took in my shapeless brown work dress and said, "I got me the prettiest calicos on bolts in the back. Would you like to take a look?"

I didn't respond. I was trying to work out how I might pay for something shiny new, and what, if anything, I even needed.

"Come this way, ma'am. Let me show you. I can open up the back and you can take a look. Pretty much whatever you need, I got."

"You're not from around here, are you?"

"No'm, I'm not. I'm from Ohio, actually, but I was making my way west to see what there is to see, and a man offered me this rig for a cheap price. I figured I should try my hand at merchandising, so here I am."

I nodded my head as I walked past an unmatched pair of tired-looking horses hitched to the front. Their heads were hanging low, and they took turns sighing deeply as they stood waiting.

"He gave me the territory, but I'm expanding on it. I want to bring goods direct to more farmin' families like yourself."

"Oh."

"What are you needin', ma'am?" his tone was patient, as if I were a child.

I looked at him like he was from the moon. His questions were so alien to me. My decisions had been made for me my whole life by my parents, and now by my husband. I don't believe I was ever before asked what I needed, let alone wanted.

"What are you wantin'?" he just looked at me expectantly. "I probably have what you be wantin'."

I had no idea what I might be wantin', and I wondered whether he really would be able to fulfill my desires were I to come to know any.

As the stranger opened his rig to me, I noticed that his hands were very clean, and his nails were neatly trimmed. Oliver had difficulty getting the dirt out from under his nails. I peered inside, and I was amazed by all the pretty things he had to show me. Maybe he really could help me find something I might need.

"I can help you, ma'am. I can help you figure out what you need."

How did he do that? It was like he listened in on my private thoughts and put voice to them. It scared me a little. I moved a step away from him.

He reached into the back of his wagon and drew out a bolt of pretty blue cotton fabric. He moved closer to me so I could see the pretty floral and feather pattern in the material. Maybe I'd be able to make myself a new dress. I hadn't bothered to make myself anything fresh in a while.

"The blue would be real pretty with your blue eyes and your dark hair, ma'am."

I felt my face redden as if he'd paid me a compliment. I took a step away from him.

"I don't need anything right now, uh…"

"Mr. Ziglar's m'name, ma'am," he reminded me. "Why don't you talk it over with your husband tonight? See what he might be needin' and I'll return tomorrow."

He put the bolt of cloth away neatly and refastened the doors on the wagon. Tipping his top hat to me, he climbed up in front and clucked at the horses to wake them up and let them know it was time to move again. Slapping the reins on their backs, he bade me farewell.

"Until tomorrow, then, Mrs. Franklin," and he drove down the drive toward the road that led into town.

I was stopped in my tracks. For some reason, I felt breathless and disoriented.

"Now what was I doing?" I said aloud as I returned to the kitchen to free the loaves of bread from their pans to cool in the open window.

I didn't purchase any fabric from Mr. Ziglar that first meeting, but I was prepared to buy enough of that blue cotton material to make myself a new dress when he turned up again late in the next spring season.

He came along in his top hat, perched on the high seat of his peddler's wagon behind a matched set of spirited Morgans. Gone were the tired two from last year. It was an unlikely pairing of elegant horses pulling a squeaky, worn out, wooden contraption with metal wares hanging from the sides. In time, I learned that he had traded his mismatched horses and a bolt of cloth to a widow woman in Kansas who wanted calmer horses to hitch to her buggy. She cared not that they didn't match each other.

Mr. Ziglar came to sell me a wash tub, and I had no way to anticipate how much an itinerant salesman could charm me.

Each year that he came and parked by the barn for a spell, he learned about each of us, and we learned a bit more about him. He was special to my children, and they would talk about him or mention him in their conversations even months after he had gone down the road to the next family. I never spoke of him to anyone, but I thought of him more and more each year after he left us to go on to the next region.

Being without a family or a permanent home allowed Mr. Ziglar the luxury of time and solitude which he could spend as he pleased. He told me that he chose to occupy his spare time in reading. He traded books as he made his rounds of the prairie territories he served over the course of a year. He was very organized and had a set and mapped route that he inherited from the peddler man from whom he bought the wagon.

The books he read took Mr. Ziglar much farther afield than the vast inland prairie he rolled through day after day. He read philosophy, and before my father-in-law, Mr. Franklin, moved to southwestern Nebraska with his new wife, he loved to come by to discuss the ideas of German philosophers with Mr. Ziglar. Mr. Franklin couldn't read or write, but his mind was sharp, and the concepts Mr. Ziglar had introduced to him the year before had stayed clearly in his mind. When the peddler came back around, Mr. Franklin made a point of stopping at our place, and they were able to pick up where their conversation had taken them the last time, as if it had just been the day before.

Oliver liked getting Mr. Ziglar's crop reports from other regions he had passed through in the season. They would talk about new farming methods or technologies and share a smoke, surveying the horizon or the fields in a companionable silence. My husband and Mr. Ziglar clamped their teeth down on their pipes as they held fresh matches to the bowls from time to time and pulled deeply on the sweet tobacco burning inside.

Over the years, Mr. Ziglar recited poetry to us from memory. I might have heard a couple of the poems before, but I didn't have any idea who had written them, even if he had told me the last time. There were many poems he would recite off the top of his head, stating the author's name at the conclusion.

There were the silly ditties he recited for the children, like the one questioning who made the little lamb ("Blake"). He described epic adventures to the older boys, like the one about a traveler he'd met who described a fallen king decaying in the middle of a desert ("Shelley"). There was a thrilling one about tiger eyes burning bright in the dark night ("Blake" again).

And then there were the poems that were not silly that he recited for me alone. I wasn't sure whether he was teasing me, or chiding me, or trying to seduce me, or all at the same time, when he began to recite Shakespeare's sonnets to me.

One morning when the children and Oliver had all left us to start their day, he began with "Here's one for you, Mrs. Franklin.":

Weary with toil, I haste me to my bed,
The dear repose for limbs with travel tired,
But then begins a journey in my head
To work my mind when body's work's expired;
For then my thoughts, from far where I abide,
Intend a zealous pilgrimage to thee,

And keep my drooping eyelids open wide,
Looking on darkness when the blind to see;
Save that my soul's imaginary sight
Presents thy shadow to my sightless view,
Which, like a jewel hung in ghastly night,
Makes black night beauteous and her old face new.
 Lo, thus, by day my limbs, by night my mind,
 For thee and for myself no quiet find.

"Shakespeare, number 26."

He paused a bit longer on words like 'bed' and 'thee'. My face felt hot. It made me want to run outside to busy myself with a chore. His reading held my attention even though I knew it shouldn't. I didn't look at him even when I knew he was looking at me, but I stayed to listen, and I allowed him to keep speaking.

As I weeded the garden, or kneaded the bread dough, I imagined him in his solitary travels, journeying from place to place. When I ironed or mended, I thought of him lying alone at night reading, as he did, in bed by lamplight. I only knew of this because he described the bed in his wagon as his favorite place where he found comfort, refuge, and rest.

There was no one I ever would have shared these thoughts with, for surely they were impure. What made them impure was when I would insert myself into the picture with him. When I was alone in the house, I fantasized that he would read sweet and passionate words to me, passages that moved my heart and transported my soul. And my stomach tingled deep inside when I'd wonder what it would feel like for him to embrace me and cover my mouth with his, allowing him to take my body slowly, gently, as he'd taken my mind: with thought and care and consideration.

I had never experienced consideration in my marital bed. I was happy to provide for my husband's needs, but he had no idea how to tend to mine. I don't believe Oliver even realized I had any needs. He must have thought that his satisfaction was mine as well, but he never thought to ask me if I was satisfied. In time, I learned to make the most of the situation for my own pleasure.

His redemption was that Oliver did hold me as we fell asleep. That was my comfort as it was his. He was not one to express any emotion, but in the moments when he reached for me in the night, I felt I was foremost in his heart.

Those of my children left at home were all old enough by the fall of 1911 to fend for themselves. They proved as much when I was lost in the haze of mourning my youngest daughter.

My sweet girl, Clara Grace, left us in the warm spring, as the flowers were at their height of glory, just before the sun's cruel rays would burn too hot and make them wither.

I had named Gracie for my little sister, in light of the healing that our time together had brought me, and in the hopes that this little girl would confirm my faith in a righteous God. A faith that the survival of my two older girls, Vinnie and Belle, had justified.

My faith continued to be tested.

We had just celebrated her fifth birthday as the old year turned to a new one. We all cherished little Grace. She was our precious baby. It had been 23 years since our last angel, Bessie, flew to heaven, but Gracie's death brought me to mourning my first girls, Jessie and Bessie, all over again like it was yesterday. My chest was heavy with the compounded grief for all three of my girls. I felt it even more sharply than before.

Every season brought a fresh reminder of my absent girls. We never acknowledged their birthdays or death days like we celebrated our living children's special days. They got swats on the behind or pinches from the older boys, but the girls gave kisses instead. The day was always sweetened with a treat of their choosing, either a pie or a cake that we could all enjoy together after dinner.

All the long years without them, I had imagined Jessie and Bessie growing up alongside their brothers and sisters, learning new things, gaining new skills, feeling new emotions. They would be 24 and 26 now, probably married like my eldest James. Like their younger sister, Vinnie, they would be mothers themselves. Gracie, just five and a half, would join them in my imagination.

The thoughts just struck me out of the blue. "Bessie would be starting school now," or "Jessie would be helping me with (whatever chore I was doing) now," or "Jessie's hair would be long like Vinnie's now," or "Bessie would be getting married, too," or "having babies, too."

When those thoughts first came to my mind, I tried to share them with Oliver, but he just shook his head at me and said, "Don't do that, Lydia."

It never occurred to me to ask him why not.

When Vinnie's first baby was born, I wondered how many other grandchildren I was missing out on and how old they would be and what they would look like. I had to excuse myself and leave their company to regain my composure. It frustrated me that I got so emotional, and I was embarrassed by it.

If I let a tear escape down my cheek before I had left the room, Oliver would get upset. "Now what's wrong, Lydia? There you go again. Always crying for no good reason. What am I supposed to do about it, Lydia?"

He became so exasperated by my emotions that I didn't want to share them with him. That was another sadness I bore because when we were first married, he was the only one I was ever able to share my emotions with and feel safe. Over time, I didn't feel safe sharing with him either.

I watched how even my youngest boys were self-sufficient during my time of deepest mourning for Gracie, and my older children showed how they could care for their younger siblings. They all knew how to tend the garden, and set up the winter stores of food, and care for the animals, and the house, and help their father in the fields. I realized that I was not essential to the efficient running of our farm.

I thought about releasing myself from it. And then I turned from that idea, disappointed by my own selfishness. I must surely be the only woman in Seward County who ever considered leaving her husband and children just because. There was no good reason for it. Where would I go, and what would I do for money? I was provided for and protected. Our family was God-fearing, hard-working, productive, and contributing. We were respected in the community. But something always made me go back to the idea of being free of it all.

I was ashamed of my thoughts, and I would never consider telling anyone. What would Mama think? I wouldn't want her to think I was ungrateful for my life. What would Clary and Dutch and Amy think? I didn't want them to know I was so unhappy. My sisters surely thought that I was so blessed, like they were, with loving husbands and good children.

Maybe I was more like our crazy sister, Minnie, than I knew. Did she want to escape her functional life, too? Had she tried to leave her husband and their boys? Is that why he had put her away? That shed a new light on my younger sister's situation. We all felt sorry for her long-suffering husband, Will. But now I wondered whether we should actually be sympathetic to Minnie's plight. I felt powerless in my life, but at least my husband had not committed me to an institution.

There was nothing that could have been done to save our little Gracie, the doctor told us.

The minister said that surely there was a silver lining in the midst of the tragedy of one so young being taken back by God. He assured us she was safe in the arms of Jesus. I knew that already. Where else would she be?

But as for God, I didn't want any more to do with Him. Oliver continued to take the children to Sunday services, but I stayed behind and spent the morning thinking of my baby instead.

Feeding the chickens, baking my pies, even hanging wash on the line, were all times when I thought of her. I also thought of how else I might be spending my time. Where else could I be? Who else could I be with?

Mr. Ziglar loomed large in my thoughts. At first, I resisted, ashamed of thinking about another man besides my husband in the ways that I did. But I guess in time, I did it often enough that I wasn't ashamed of myself anymore. Besides, who would ever know? I didn't ever say a word about it to anyone. Not even my sister, Grace, who I shared everything with, since she lived close to me.

The traveling man's salt-and-pepper hair was thinning on top, and he had a soft jaw line. His shoulders were a bit hunched over from hours of sitting behind his team holding the reins with his elbows resting on his knees all day. Because he had to move his inventory around his wagon, his hands were callused, but his muscles were not very developed. Mr. Ziglar was not as physically attractive to me as my Oliver, but his intellect and his attention engaged me on a much deeper level than I had ever been engaged by anyone before.

Mr. Ziglar was not just talking at me as Oliver and Mr. Franklin, and even my own father had always done. He spoke with me, asking me questions even as he opened the world to me through his stories, both fictional and true. His questions forced me to consider what I thought about an event, or where I stood on an issue. Imagine a man consulting with a woman on any topic. It wasn't anything I was used to.

When we conversed, I felt smart, for he never criticized or laughed at anything I said even though I'd only gone to the sixth grade in school. If I didn't have a clear sense of something, his questions would guide my thoughts until I had come to a conclusion on my own and was able to clearly state my ideas to him. And he listened to my ideas like they were very important.

The poems Mr. Ziglar shared with me became softer over the years. Through them, he reached into my aching heart somehow and touched my sense of solitude and longing. It was late summer one day, when I told Mr. Ziglar my father had just passed away three months to the day after our little girl Gracie.

Tears stung my eyes and my throat tightened when, in response, he simply recited to me something about seeing into the life of things and the sad music of humanity bringing one into the presence of the divine. "Wordsworth." I turned away until I knew I could speak.

He was sitting at the head of our kitchen table. When he had taken that particular chair, it startled me a bit to see another man sitting in the place my husband usually sat. I liked it. I liked him sitting in that seat.

I took in a bracing breath as I walked toward the sink and asked him, "Are you hungry? I did something with the peaches and berries I picked this morning."

"You know I won't turn down your cooking, Mrs. Franklin."

Our eyes met then for the first time for more than a polite few seconds, and it sent a jolt of electricity from my chest downward through my body. The thought crossed my mind that he had looked through my eyes and into my lonely mind, my broken heart, and my yearning soul. I felt he understood me and knew my secrets. I looked away again and quickly placed a plate of cobbler on the table in front of him. Feeling myself blush, I turned away. What silly thoughts I have.

"Mrs. Franklin?"

My back was still to him. "Yes?"

"'*But those tears are pearls that your love sheds, and they are rich with redemption*'... or something like that. Shakespeare."

I just looked over my shoulder at him. The openness and sincerity his face showed me as he met my gaze captivated me. I couldn't look away until he broke the moment by looking down at the food I'd made.

"In all of Nebraska, I swear there isn't a better cobbler maker than you, Mrs. Franklin! I can't wait to dig in!"

When I returned to his side to place a fork on his plate, I took a deep breath and met his gaze again as he looked up at me, and I didn't shy away that time, either, for I believed I could see him as clearly as he could see me, and I liked what I saw.

After watching my husband at Gracie's grave, I knew that he suffered as I did. Oliver and I grieved for our little girl together but alone, and we were never able to fully reestablish the unspoken connection I felt we once had.

I didn't believe that he could really know me without understanding my pain. If that was the case, I didn't know how he could really love me despite our years together and our losses. I did know that he still cared for me in his own way, and that made me think twice before I made my crazy, irrational move.

As I distracted myself from my sorrow, I thought more and more about Mr. Ziglar, escaping into the fantasy of living life on the road with him, seeing new faces and places every day. When Mr. Ziglar came to supply us with new milking pails and a sharp new set of plow blades the next year, he came with fresh sonnets memorized for me.

I knew of Shakespeare, but I didn't have any appreciation for his writing at all until Mr. Ziglar spoke his words so clearly that I understood what they meant. He said them so sweetly that they felt like honey sliding down my throat when I repeated the lines back to myself.

One in particular caught my attention.

"I don't know how it goes exactly, but it was something like this: 'Neither inner worth nor outer beauty are how you should judge yourself in the eyes of men. When you give yourself away, you can't live. You must live, not through my poems, but by your own doing.'"

That was it. He had put words to my feelings. I had given myself away, and I felt more and more that I had to break away to come back to life, to come back to myself.

I didn't even know who I was outside of my relationship with my husband and my children. This was not something I had ever discussed with anyone, and I felt so alone and strange for having such yearnings.

Mr. Ziglar saw me as no one ever had before. In that moment, I knew I must accompany him when he moved on or else I would wither and die of stagnation in my life and of a longing to know myself.

As Mr. Ziglar was preparing to leave our farm for another year, he quietly recited another sweet poem to me. He knew the words to this one by heart.

"And I would go to Patty's cot
And Patty came to me;
Each knew the other's very thought
Under the hawthorn tree....
And I'll be true for Patty's sake
And she'll be true for mine;
And I this little ballad make,
To be her valentine."

Our gazes locked together. "John Clare."

I knew the butterflies and the deep tickle I felt inside me meant something. I did not want him to leave me again. I did not want to watch yet another time his boxy wagon lumber down our tree-lined lane to the road that led to town. I wanted to be next to him on that wagon seat.

I felt reckless, bold, and daring. I wanted to go on a journey. I could think of no better companion than him.

I thought back on a conversation we'd had the year before, when he asked me, "Mrs. Franklin, have you ever heard of 'free love'?"

I was unprepared for the question, and it stopped me in my tracks.

"I can't say that I have. Dare I ask?"

It sounded like promiscuity to me, but I didn't want to say that if it wasn't about sex, so I let him fill in the blanks.

"It's not about promiscuity, Mrs. Franklin."

He must have read my mind again, or saw a particular look on my face perhaps.

"It's about freedom to have and be in loving relationships of our own choosing. Society, the government, does not need to involve itself in our personal love lives."

"I don't think I understand."

"Not to pry into your business, and you don't have to give me answers, but whose name is on the deed to this farm? Do you make any decisions about your household finances, or does Mr. Franklin take care of all that? Which of you has rights to the children?"

Suddenly, my sister Minnie came to my mind again. Did she have any choice when it came time to go to that institution, or was her husband's word the final say? Was she forced to go against her will?

Of course I had no say when it came to our finances. Oliver made all the decisions, and I had to ask him for money when I needed to buy something for the children or the house. It occurred to me that I didn't even know how to get to any of our money. Oliver provided for our family, and I relied on him to give us what we needed, like I had relied on my father to provide for us when I was growing up.

I looked at Mr. Ziglar and just nodded. "I think I understand."

"See, with free love you get to have control over your own life, and choose how you spend it, and who you spend it with."

Feeling a bit defensive, I responded, "I have a fine life, Mr. Ziglar. No one has locked me up."

"Of course not, Mrs. Franklin. I didn't mean to upset you. I just wondered if you knew of it."

Now his tone sounded defensive to me. Oh dear, I didn't want to upset him.

"I apologize Mr. Ziglar. I didn't mean to offend you."

"Well, there you go. We just got our first fight out of the way!"

He flashed a sly grin at me and winked. I couldn't help but laugh aloud, and he laughed with me.

The day I left my husband and my children, I felt a pang of guilt as I thought of Oliver coming home from the fields hungry and expecting a warm dinner but finding a cold, dark kitchen instead. My desire to break away far outweighed my need to prove myself worthy of my husband anymore.

I had to do it; for myself, or else I'd go crazy like Minnie if I didn't. Her husband Will told us he had to put her away in an institution. We never discussed it, and no one went to visit her. We were sad for her, but we were also mortified. We felt it reflected poorly on our family.

In a way, I understood my father-in-law's heart because I'd only ever known love with Oliver. I was curious, however. He was my only experience, so how could I know how deeply I really loved him? What if there was another man who I could love more? What if I missed my opportunity to discover a truly deep love; one like Dutch had with Tom, or like Amy had with Ol, where I could feel relaxed and free to do and say what I really wanted?

Although I had promised to be his wife until death, I feared I didn't love Oliver enough. Not with all the devotion of my heart, like Mr. Franklin loved Oliver's mother. There were many times I didn't think my husband really knew me. I was not sure that he really loved me, so how could I give my whole heart to him?

I convinced myself that he would not miss me. He would barely notice I was gone, since he barely seemed to notice my presence anyway.

The uncomfortable feelings of my own self-doubt and guilt were overshadowed by a sense of euphoria. I knew I was in for an adventure. I was diving headfirst off the edge and into an abyss; a deep well of sin and shame. And freedom.

Josie

LEFT US

Iheld in the warm wet for as long as I could stand it. After much time had passed, how much I do not know, darkness descended to hide the act. I was dismayed to have to do it, but finally I just released the pressure. My pink housecoat wicked it up around my hips, and it quickly became cold dampness.

The kitty, Josephine, was curious. Her pink nose twitched about my prone form. Her whiskers tickled my skin where it was bare: my legs, my hands, my face, which was wet with silent, salty tears. She clearly was not sure what to make of it. Truly, I wasn't sure what to make of it either.

I simply could not get up. One minute I was on my feet ironing in the clear light of the crisp November afternoon, and the next minute I was on my back. The wooden board lay next to me, and I was grateful the iron had gone the other direction, rather than on my head. Maybe I should unplug the iron from the wall lest it burn into the linoleum; there was no amount of scrubbing that could take a burn mark away. When I tried to roll over to get up, by body just fell back.

I lay still for a moment, and it occurred to me that my hip must be broken. Oh dear. That's the kiss of death. I knew so many whose last act was falling to the ground. No. It couldn't be that for me. I called out for help.

"Luella! Roy!"

Their house was behind mine. Maybe they could hear me. I remembered then that they were gone for the evening. My older daughter Luella had poked her head in the door as they left for a night of BINGO. I was alone, and they wouldn't be home for a while. I decided to settle in and just wait. She always checked in on me when they came in for the night.

I was very nearly done with the ironing, and the piles of fresh, smooth linens that I'd lined up on the guest bed down the hall were ready to be put away in the hall closet. The iron was still plugged in. I reached for the cord to pull it out of the wall, but it was out of reach. I tried to shimmy closer to reach it, but a searing pain stopped me. I blew my breath out in quick bursts until the pain eased up a bit.

If that iron started a fire, I'd really be done for, so I braced myself and pushed with my other foot. My body moved, and although the pain was as intense as before, I expected it, and now I knew which side was hurt. I didn't know if it was broken or not, so why borrow trouble and name a thing if it's not that thing?

Well, whatever my condition, I was in a pickle, and no one but Josephine the cat was around to lend me a hand. Big help she was to me. Yes, her name was the same as mine, and no, I did not name her myself. She came to me with that name. It was meant to be: two Josephines finding themselves paired up together after all was said and done.

I never wanted to end up alone at the end of my life. I was strong for a long time without my Lee. A widow for 17 years, I was as independent as I could be, although I relied some on Luella and Roy, and in truth, I was so lonely without a companion. It made me all the more grateful for the life we had together, and our children and all the children that have come to be because of our children, and all the children that will be because of them! And to think—I almost ended up a spinster.

People wonder how it happened that first cousins married one another in the 20th century. I know it. I remember when Nancy and Pamela, Beth's daughter and Tom's daughter, came up for a visit from California. Pamela wasn't raised with us, but obviously someone let her in on it. She asked me, "Grandma, were you and Grandpa really first cousins?"

I could see on Nancy's face that she was horrified. "Pam!" she exclaimed. Nancy had never asked me about it. She obviously had been told not to bring it up with us, but Pam had no such compunction. I smiled at her and said, "Yes we were."

Nancy quickly changed the subject, and I didn't get another opportunity to tell our story.

Everyone is always curious, and I am well aware that people talked about us when we weren't around, but most people didn't have the courage to ask us about it. If they'd have asked and listened, we'd have just told them.

I didn't know my cousin until we were already grown. We were brought up a state apart. His mama and my mama came from a large family. There were eight of them: six sisters and two brothers. That meant we all had lots of cousins, especially because two of my mother's siblings married two siblings from the Franklin family. That is the family that I also married into.

Most of my aunts and uncles moved west as we were growing up, so there were some cousins that I didn't have the opportunity to meet until we were much older. Frequent letters and of course train travel made the distances between us seem closer, but the cost of traveling, not to mention the obligations of home, kept the Papas and the children at home. Somebody had to stay and milk the cows, so we looked forward to the letters and to our aunts' visits to us.

I was 31 years old myself when I finally left Iowa in 1912 to visit them. I accompanied my Grandma Chloe when she went to see her daughters, Lydia and Grace, and their families in Nebraska. Of course, I knew my aunts from when they had come to visit us, and from their letters to us, but I had not yet met my cousins in person, aside from James.

I was so saddened the year before our visit, when I learned that the youngest sister, Gracie, had passed away. During our visit, I could tell my Aunt Lydia was still devastated by that loss even a year later. She was often lost in thought and seemed even more somber than usual. I saw Grandma Chloe watch her and try to draw her out with stories of Aunt Clary's family, or of our family in Iowa, but she was only polite and couldn't fool either one of us into believing she was interested at all.

When my cousins, Billy and Stubb, took my hand and our Grandma's hand to lead us to their three sisters' graves, which were side by side at the back of their property, Aunt Lydia didn't want to come with us. She said she had some things to do, however when we came back, we found her sitting in a rocking chair just looking out the window.

When I was 33 years old, old was how I felt. There was nowhere in my hometown of Winterset, Iowa for me to go to be independent. I certainly loved my family, but my whole life revolved around the family. I taught school and I brought my earnings home to Papa. I still had chores to do, and I tended to the animals, helped Mama with the gardening, canning, cooking, and looking after the little ones. Then I helped look after my younger sister Margaret's three little girls, and my younger brother Ray's son.

I was content to be with my family, and extended family, but it occurred to me that if I outlived everyone, I might have some trouble supporting myself as I got old with no children of my own. I helped my mother. She and her siblings helped her mother, Grandma Chloe. Who would help me when I got to be old?

I was unusual in our community. All my girlfriends had gotten married long ago. I guess I could have married, had I changed who I was. I had more than a few beaux over the years, and more than a few left me with the parting words, "You talk too much, Josie."

I was never one to keep quiet if I had an opinion. As years passed, however, I realized that not everyone should be entitled to hear my opinions and those who didn't like that I had something to say were definitely not men I wanted to devote my life to.

My cousin, Goldie, Aunt Amy's daughter, was also unmarried. Granted, she was 14 years younger than I, but as another unmarried woman, I felt she understood me. Not that she had trouble getting beaux, but she also was very opinionated and outspoken.

I got a letter one day from Goldie, telling me about something promising that she heard of in Montana. She wanted me to go. It was a training course for teachers. They were in desperate need of good teachers in Montana, and the pay was better than in Iowa, especially since I already had been a teacher for a number of years. I needed a change of scenery. A change of pace would be a good thing for me.

I thought about it for a little while, and when I'd made up my mind, I shared Goldie's letter with my mother. She did not receive the news kindly.

"Oh no, Josie. Please don't go! Montana is wilderness. It's dangerous there."

"Of course I don't want to leave you, Mama. I knew you wouldn't want me to go, but I feel like I will crawl out of my skin if I have to stay put. I have been in Iowa my entire life. Nothing changes here for me. I watch seasons come and go, yet I am still in the same place. Myrtle has been married twice already."

Myrtle was my twin cousin. She and I were born three weeks apart, and when we were little, we were inseparable until Uncle Hi and Aunt Dora moved out to Nebraska with Aunt Lydia and Uncle Oliver and his family. They returned home to Iowa 5 years later, but they weren't in Madison County anymore. Then they moved every couple of years after that. Myrtle got married when we were 19, and our lives continued to go in different directions. I *wanted* to be married and have a family. She *was* married and had a family.

"I feel ready for a change. Papa understands me. He thinks maybe it would be a good thing."

Mama was digging in her special wooden letter box while I was speaking, so I got the feeling she hadn't heard a word I said. I was mistaken.

"Just like your Papa to release my chickadees into the wilderness and call it a good thing. Now you just listen to this, Josie. This is from your Aunt Amy."

I felt impatient, but just picked up my glass from the table, took a sip of cool water, and prayed silently for Jesus to give me patience.

"Amy says her Goldie wrote her a letter recently and here's what it says. 'Dear Mamma, I'm almost scared to death every morning now. There are a timber wolf and a lynx crossing my road to school every night.'"

Mama looked at me over her reading spectacles.

"'Guess I'll get me an automatic 6-gun today. For it is really dangerous.'"

She enunciated each word so I would understand the significance of her message.

"'The wild animals are mighty hungry, and so many have the rabies. I run nearly all the way to school.' Now what do you think of that, Josie?"

"Goldie is in a country school, Mama. Just because I'm going to Montana doesn't mean they are all country schools."

"But you don't like guns, Josie, and you'd have to get one."

"No, Mama. I wouldn't necessarily have to get a gun. I'll be staying with Aunt Amy and Uncle Ol. I'll be safe."

"Hmph. Now listen to what else Goldie told her mother. 'I almost had a scrap at school the other day, but one of the kids suddenly discovered who was "boss".' And Amy says that she hurt her shoulder. You can't be fighting with those children, Josie. The boys will be bigger than you."

"I won't be fighting with anyone, Mama. Have I ever gotten into a fight with a pupil in any of my schools here?"

"Well, no."

"Please let me go, Mama. I promise to write all the time."

"I don't like it, Josie."

"Dutch. She is a grown woman, and she knows her own mind."

Papa's stern voice startled Mama, and she tucked the letter away and put her box back in its place.

"I didn't hear you come in, Tom."

"Let her go, Dutch."

"You don't seem to understand, Thomas. There are dangers."

Papa looked at me and winked one blue eye. I smiled at him, relieved and grateful, for I knew there would be no more discussion about it. From a lifetime of observation, I knew that in such debates, while Mama may have had the last word, Papa always had the final say.

"Montana will be a good thing. I would be scared of the long journey if I didn't have Goldie and Aunt Amy waiting on the other end for me."

I was reassuring my little sister Edith who, like Mama, was begging me to stay. It was also a secret reassurance for myself. If I were honest, I'd admit that beneath my excitement there was a bit of fear.

"What shall I do without my big sissie, Josie?"

I gave her a hug and promised to write. When I went up the steps into the train car, I heard Mama crying behind me. I turned to see Papa standing behind them with a big hand on each of their shoulders. My mother held a handkerchief to her face with one hand and waved to me with the other.

"Love you all."

"More than tongue can tell."

My family's voices called back to me in unison and echoed sweetly in my mind as I found a seat with the conductor's help. I settled in to watch the passing landscape out the window. I was glad I brought the quilt Mama and Grandma Chloe made me, for the air was cool around me.

There were many people on the train. Families, other women who appeared to travel in pairs, men traveling alone. Children walked, sometimes ran, back and forth, until their parents called them to sit in one place. After a while, I took out my correspondence pad and a pencil, and I began a letter to Mama and Papa. I didn't have much to say, since I had just left them, so I flipped that paper over and started a fresh letter.

This one was to Aunt Grace in Nebraska. So close in age, we were more like cousins than aunt and niece. I hoped she and Uncle Frank and the kids were doing well, and asked how was the garden and their chickens? I let her know I was on a train to Montana to meet up with Goldie and enter a program to become a teacher there. I told her I left Mama and the family in good health, if not in good spirits. I told her how excited I was to be having an adventure and was hoping to hear back from her at Aunt Amy's in Montana just as soon as she could spare a minute to write me. I signed it, "Love, Josie."

I didn't sleep much through the night as the train progressed at a steady pace across the vast, open western lands. The lights were off in the car, and most of the other passengers were managing to get some sleep. I heard some of their snores even over the noise of the wheels on the tracks. As I looked out the window, I could see a bit of the land-scape that the bright moon illuminated. Mostly shadows outside, the light helped cut the darkness inside. The occasional passerby nodded at me when they saw I was also awake as they made their way to the toilets and back to their seats again.

I watched the sunrise light come up on the blacks, grays, and mut-ed tones, until the land was in full color and I could clearly see the tall grass and the clusters of tree tops in low river valleys that moved past my smudged window.

Aunt Amy and Uncle Ol were at the station awaiting my arrival, and I was so relieved to see familiar faces after my two-day journey. Goldie was off teaching at her school in Plains, where she stayed with the family of one of her pupils. I would see her when she came home for term break in a few weeks.

I settled in right away with my new schedule, and before I knew it, I had my own school, with my very own pupils. Because I had so much experience, and my test scores were higher than other candidates, the Board of Trustees wanted me to teach in the town school. That was good for me because I got to stay with Aunt Amy and Uncle Ol.

They were a rough and tumble crowd, my little flock. Sweet helpful girls, and dirty-faced puppy-dog boys. The mischievous Whitcomb brothers gave me grief, but then one would set an apple on my desk, and that always cheered me. A photographer came by one day and took our picture on the schoolhouse steps. I sent it to my cousin, Belle, in Nebraska, and told her as much about my students as would fit on the back.

"*They are just ordinary children, of course, but they all look pretty good to me, except the Whitcombs. They are the ones in front with dirty faces and their caps on. The boy sitting next to the building with his cap on is Roy Brown. He is a cute little fellow, but he was so busy getting as far from the girls as possible, that he forgot to take off this hat. The one just in front of him on the banister is Harold Morris, our fine speller. Isn't he scholarly looking? The girl who stood next to me said she guessed she was winking at the photographer. The boy on the end with such rough hair was writing exams that day. This is how he always fixed his hair, to think well.*"

In the letter to Belle, I also asked about the family; whether Lee was still playing baseball. I wondered about Aunt Lydia, but I dared not ask a thing about it. If Belle wanted to say anything, she would.

When I asked Mother why we hadn't heard from her sister in a while, she said that she didn't know. The fact was, no one knew anything except Mama, and all she knew, that she told me, was that Uncle Oliver had written asking whether Lydia was with us, or if we had heard from her. She reminded me we'd best not say anything in front of Grandma Chloe to cause her undue upset. Aunt Lydia's sudden disappearance one day from her home was a mystery. I know Mama worried, but she refused to speculate or gossip about her sister.

"When there is something to know, we'll know."

The only clue she had left behind was a brief note, which assured us she was still alive at least.

I got a letter one day, but it wasn't from my best friend Rose, or from Aunt Grace, or from my cousin Belle, or even from Mama, begging me to "please come home, Josie." This one was from Belle's big brother, Lee.

I recalled the day Lee and I had met for the first time a couple of years before when I accompanied Grandma Chloe on the train to Seward, Nebraska for a week-long June visit at Aunt Lydia and Uncle Oliver's place. When they left Iowa for Nebraska, their oldest boy, James, was not yet three, and I wasn't but a year older than him, but when he greeted me, he felt familiar, and I gave him a big bear hug.

I'd known about them all through letters Aunt Lydia sent to Grandma Chloe and to Aunt Clary and to Mama, but I met my other cousins for the first time that day. There were hugs and laughter all around at the train station with those who came to greet us and then carry us back to their farm in the wagon.

When we pulled into the yard, Uncle Oliver came out of the barn to say hello and then another young man followed behind him. I don't know why, but I couldn't quite catch my breath. I liked the looks of him. He was tall and lean, with curly auburn hair that just couldn't be completely controlled and twinkling blue eyes.

"Lee!"

He bent down to embrace our Grandma Chloe in a warm, gentle hug.

"Grandma! You're even more beautiful than the last time I saw you!"

"Oh, say more, you sweet talker!"

We all laughed and then he straightened up and turned to greet me. He suddenly seemed shy with me, but I smiled at him, and he stepped right up and gave me a hug that took my breath away.

"Josie!"

He held me at arm's length, resting his hands on my shoulders, and looked me square in the eye. I responded in kind.

"Lee!"

He winked at me, and I giggled. His lips curled into a wry, flirty smile. My stomach was all aflutter. I glanced over my shoulder to get another look at him as I followed the other women into the house. I reached into my bag and found my apron, which I put on to help get dinner on the table.

Lee was just 19 and I was 31, but he made me laugh, and I felt light and young around him. There was a sense of familiarity we shared, an inexplicable feeling of closeness that was immediate and deeper than with the others, although I spent equal time with each of my other cousins.

Ernest had a camera, and we had fun getting our pictures made on the day we arrived and then on the day we left. I never saw those pictures until Lee put one of them in his letter to me. It showed Lee with his arms over Belle's and my shoulders. I had on my blue crossover waist that I traveled in. Lee looked quite natty with his bow tie and his curls slicked down as much as they could be. Belle had a big bow in her hair.

I remembered how we went to a couple of professional baseball games that week. Grandma Chloe and Aunt Lydia stayed behind to put up some fresh peach preserves and do some mending, but the rest of us made our way out to the baseball grounds with Uncle Oliver, and we watched the local team play the visiting team whose name I couldn't recall. I also couldn't tell you who won those games. I didn't really care, to be honest. All I knew about baseball was that I enjoyed watching the games.

It felt good to be outside in the sunshine and fresh air. I breathed in the smell of the sweet, newly-cut grass, and listened for the satisfying crack of the wooden bat against the ball. It was exciting to see the runners rounding the bases and the dust clouds rise under their feet as the crowd cheered them on.

Lee brought a baseball and threw it around with his younger brothers, Billy and Stubb, after the game. The boys were all good throwers, but Lee's pitches seemed particularly strong to me.

I was happy to receive Lee's letter. He said Belle and Aunt Grace had shared my letters with the family, and he was taken aback that I'd left home and journeyed so far to teach.

"Don't they have schools in Iowa that you can be a 'marm at?"

I smiled, in spite of the preposition at the end of his sentence. Of course they do.

Lee and I wrote back and forth several times. I told him about my pupils and kept him up to date with what was happening with Aunt Amy and Uncle Ol, and with what I knew from letters from Mama and my sisters back home. He filled me in on his endeavors.

In his next letter, Lee told me that he went to play for the Grand Island Collegians, the very team we had watched play when Grandma Chloe and I visited his family in Nebraska.

Even though I didn't know much about the game, I could imagine Lee on the pitching mound, sending strikes over the home plate. I also saw him in my mind's eye running around the bases after hitting the ball into the far outfield, like he and his brothers did after we watched the professionals play.

His older brothers, James and Ernest, had both played professional ball as well, so Lee said he guessed it was becoming a family tradition because both Billy and Stubb said they also wanted to play ball professionally. When he wasn't playing ball, Lee helped his father on the farm.

As it turned out, the team didn't have him back the next season, so Lee went to play for the York Prohibitionists. It was better, he wrote, since the new team was just a bit closer to home. Then he wrote something that surprised me.

"I've been thinking of going to Montana to learn the logging business."

Well, I thought, *wouldn't that be something if he got a logging job close to my school.*

Next thing I knew, there was Lee knocking on my classroom door. I was just finishing marking some papers after the children left school for the day. I looked up to see his smiling face. I was so surprised, I started to laugh, and for some reason a blush rose up on my face.

He came over and caught me up in a big hug in his rock-solid strong arms and twirled me around against his long, lean body.

"Josie! How've you been? Told ya I'd be coming to Montana, and now here I am!"

He put me back on the ground, but my stomach felt like it was still in flight. He held my hands in his and stepped back, assessing my appearance. I was surely a bit disheveled after a day of teaching and being swung around.

"Well, schoolmarm, you're a sight for sore eyes! I've been in the forest for a couple of weeks learning the ropes, and you're the first lady I've set eyes on since then."

"What are you doing here, Lee? It's so good to see you."

"Finally got a day off, and couldn't decide how to spend it, so I figured I'd pay a visit to my favorite cousin, Josie!"

I smiled at him and squeezed his hands.

"I'm glad you found me, Lee!"

"I had some help. Had to ask a few people. You hungry? I think we should get something to eat."

"Yes. I am."

So that was when it started. When we were both working, we wrote letters back and forth. When he had a day off every few weeks, Lee would spend it with me. We might hire a rig and go out to visit Goldie at her cabin, or stay in town to take a meal with Aunt Amy and Uncle Ol. Then we'd walk to the square to hear the municipal band play. Most often we went out for a drive in the countryside, down to the river, or up to the foothills with a picnic lunch. Lee always had a ball that we might throw around, and we'd walk in the fields and put our feet in the cold streams.

I began to miss his company when he wasn't with me. Then one day he told me he missed me when I wasn't with him. Lee didn't feel like just a cousin to me when I was with him. He didn't feel like just a friend. My feelings ran deeper somehow. I wanted to be caught up in his embrace and stay there always.

One day after lunch, we lay on a blanket side by side watching puffy white clouds floating past in the deep blue sky. I was quieter than usual, and he tried to tease what was on my mind out of me.

"You don't have another beau you're missing, do you, Josie?"

"No, Lee. You are my only beau."

I looked at him to see what his reaction would be, and I was surprised when he got serious with me.

"I am?" He propped himself up on his elbows.

"Yes, Lee, you are." I sat up, and then he sat up facing me.

I took his hands and looked at them, waiting for what he would say. When I met his gaze, he asked me, "Josie, do you feel about me the way I feel about you?" His wide eyes searched my face.

"I don't know, Lee. How do you feel about me?"

I feared his answer, but I wanted to know it more than I didn't, whichever way he felt.

We had talked about everything together. We compared childhood experiences, and talked about people that we knew in common, being related and all.

We shared our thoughts about the recently elected President Wilson. "I don't trust him as far as I can throw him," said Lee.

"Why ever not?" I was surprised by his passion.

"I can't put my finger on it. Maybe it's because he's southern, or Presbyterian, or... oh I don't know."

"I like him. He has three daughters, and his mother was Scottish, like my Papa. He seems to care about the country. I like how he calls himself the leader of all people, not just the leader of one group's cause."

"Well, I didn't vote for him." He looked at me with a straight face, and I started to giggle.

"Of course not, Lee. You were only 19 at the election. I didn't either," I said with a frown, since by law, I wasn't allowed to vote, being a woman and all. We both started to giggle again.

When we laughed at the same things, which was often, I felt our bond deepen.

We couldn't know it at the time, but I would get to vote for the first time five years later in the 1920 election, thanks to the 19th Constitutional amendment that was passed during Wilson's second term. It gave women suffrage in our country.

We missed our families, sharing correspondence we were sending home, and reading the letters we were receiving from them. He had even brought up his mother going away without a word to the family. Lee would write to Belle, "Any word on Mother?" and she would answer simply, "No word on Mother."

He wondered if their mother was all right, and whether she'd be back. He said the worry of not knowing stayed with him.

We had discussed what we wanted for our lives. He wanted to have a family, and I said that I did, too.

He hadn't gone to school much past the sixth grade, but he wasn't uncomfortable with the fact that I was a schoolteacher. That didn't intimidate him. Nothing did. He loved people, and he was happy for other people's successes.

He told me more about his season pitching for the Grand Island Collegians, the year after my visit. He told me how elated he was when he pitched a winning game, and how disappointed he was when the team let him go. He wasn't resentful, though. He wished his old teammates well.

Lee was buoyant and resilient. He sought and found the next thing, which was logging.

He and a few of the guys made their time on the job fun, although he said it was the hardest work he'd ever done, and it was upsetting to him when a guy got hurt. I learned that when he came to visit, if he was affected by something that had happened on the job, to just be with him and not ask too many questions.

"Jones rolled off a log today," Lee said one day with a somber tone.

"What does that mean?" I asked, picturing a man lying on a log and rolling off it to the ground.

"He was on a log in the river, and it rolled. We couldn't find him."

"Are you saying he drowned?"

"When the raftsmen move the logs down the river, they are on the logs. When a log gets loose, it can spin within a log jam, but those guys know how to walk on the logs. Jones slipped."

"So… he was trapped under the logs?"

Lee just nodded. He always spared me the gory details, but it made me nervous for his safety if I let myself think about it, so I was grateful not to know too much.

"You don't walk on logs, do you, Lee?"

"No," he reassured me. "I am not a raftsman. I don't want to die that way!"

"Good! I don't want you to die at all!"

Lee did talk a lot about how the new guys on the job always had to survive a gauntlet of tests thought up by the other loggers. He told me that he saw them put dirt, or worse, into the coffee of one new man. The old hands always made the new ones do the hardest, dirtiest jobs, while they just watched and laughed.

Exhausted new hires would try to get into bunks where the sheets had been tucked in half, so they couldn't even get in. They'd have to take it all apart and remake the bed so they could sleep in it. Some were so spent, they just gave up and slept on top, freezing through the cold night.

Lee said, "If I didn't laugh as much at myself, they'd probably haze me as much as the other new hires!"

He did get hazed, though. One of his first days on the job, he said that they made him climb a particularly tall tree, for he had made the mistake of letting them know he didn't feel so good when he was too high off the ground. To get back at them, after their shift, Lee ran back to the mess hall and gathered up all the forks and put them somewhere out of sight, except one. Lee was the only one eating with a fork that night, and when the men realized what he had done, they roared with laughter. He never had to go up another tall tree again. Lee could give as good as he got, and from what he told me, it seemed that the other men respected him for it.

I thought Lee was wonderful, and some woman was going to be lucky to be his wife. I dared not even consider that it could be me. Well, not a whole lot anyway.

"I love you, Josie!"

"I love you, too, Lee, but I think I'm talking about a different kind of love."

"I hope not. My love is completely inappropriate, and our parents wouldn't approve if they knew about it."

"What do you mean, Lee?"

"Am I going to have to spell it out for you? I love you. I don't like being away from you. You make me feel happy. I am calm when I am around you. You feel like home to me, Josie. I want to feel like that always."

"But we are already family."

"I know that. But I want to really be family with you, Josie. I want to make a family with you."

My stomach did a somersault, and my toes tingled.

"You do?"

"Yes."

We just stared at each other for a minute. Were we about to jump off a cliff together? That's what it felt like to me.

"Do you know how old I am, Lee?"

"No, and I don't care how old you are. To me, you are perfect, whatever your age."

"But I am old."

"Not in my eyes you're not. And I get lost in your eyes. Time stands still when I look into those beautiful blue pools, and there's nowhere else I want to be. I think of your eyes every day, Josie, when I'm not with you. I imagine them to help me fall asleep at night."

I felt my face get hot, and I knew it had turned red, but I couldn't wait to hear more from him.

"Did you know that you're the last thing I think of as I drift off to sleep?"

"No I did not. Am I?"

For some reason, I couldn't bring myself to tell him he was also the last thing I thought of. I just smiled at this new information. Maybe loving him wasn't as crazy as I thought after all. That, or we'd be crazy together.

"Did you know that I have to share a bunk with another man?"

I was surprised by this added detail, but only shook my head.

"How else do you think I can tolerate that, Josie? You give me something to think about other than the fact that I'm under a blanket with a smelly man with cold feet that stray to my side every night. You're saving me by being the love of my life!"

I laughed. He laughed. Our laughter calmed my nerves. I could breathe.

"So what do you say, Josie? Will you marry me and spend the rest of your life with me?"

I was quite taken aback. Tears sprang to my eyes, and my throat closed so tight, I couldn't speak. I didn't even think. I just nodded my head and took a deep breath.

"Yes, Lee. I'll marry you."

His smile became even wider, and he pulled me close in a big bear hug. And then he kissed me. He stopped to look into my eyes. He must have seen what he was looking for because he kissed me again, slowly, deeply, holding me closer to him.

What had I just done? I'd promised to share my life with this young man, who was so handsome and dashing and funny. Who did I think I was to claim him for myself? What would our families say? I was a bit embarrassed, thinking about it. He was so much younger. Were we perverted? He was my cousin. Was I being selfish? I couldn't bear the thought of letting him go. He said he loved me.

Then I felt another wave of calm wash over me, and the questions just stopped. The misgivings had all gone. What was that, I wondered? The answer just came into my mind. Oh, it was relief. I wouldn't be alone after all.

Thank God.

We made plans to get married right away, as Lee didn't even want to wait another day. We did wait a few days, until my summer teaching contract in Montana ended at the end of that week.

I had planned to go back to Iowa soon anyway, and Lee was ready to leave lumber-jacking and head home just in time to help his father on the farm for the autumn harvest season. Lee had saved some money, so we felt ready to start a new life together somewhere between our family homes.

Belle had written Lee to tell him that there was a machinist in Lincoln looking for an assistant, and he was asking specifically for Lee. Lee wrote back right away and told her that he was coming, and please tell the man to hold the job for him.

Lee decided we should travel to Colorado in the used jalopy he'd recently bought and get married there. It took several days on bumpy road, and when we set out, I was very nervous about how we would spend the nights. I was relieved and grateful when Lee took it upon himself to get a separate room for each of us.

I did not want to give in to the temptation I already experienced on our outings alone in the countryside. We agreed it would only ruin what we knew would be a sweet and sacred moment for us once we had been married in the eyes of God.

Montana and Nebraska had laws against marrying couples who were related as closely as Lee and I; however, Nebraska would recognize our marriage if it was formalized in a state where it was legal. We made a brief wedding stop in Wray, Colorado, where we found a minister to marry us in his parlor with his wife and teen-aged daughter standing by to witness for us.

After the ceremony, we stopped at a diner for a light lunch, but we realized that neither one of us had much of an appetite. We left our half-eaten plates and crossed the street to the hotel where we nervously got a room together for the night.

All that needs to be said about sharing a bed with my new husband for the first time is that it was a bit awkward, and it was tender and surprising, and then once he fell asleep, it was loud. I did manage to get some sleep, although he snored in my ear as he cuddled in close behind me with his arm cradling me.

In the gray light of dawn, we awoke together, our naked bodies entwined and already aroused. We were able then to cast aside our awkwardness and get past the surprise of it all to experience the fullness of our enjoyment of each other as man and wife without inhibition and without shame.

We found our appetites again, after which we had a hearty breakfast at our leisure at the same diner from the day before. Then we set out ready to face our family together.

We had a long road ahead of us and nothing but time, so without my having to ask any questions, Lee started talking.

"She was just gone one day. We all came home, and Mom wasn't there. She left a note on the kitchen table. All it said was, 'I have to go.'"

My husband looked at me, to get my reaction I guessed, but I didn't say a word. I just looked back at him and waited for him to continue.

"I don't like to talk about it, Josie, and I'm only telling you because you are my wife now, and you should know."

"Darling, you know I won't breathe a word of this to anyone."

"I'm sorry, I just had to say it."

He took a moment to gather his thoughts, and he took a few deep breaths.

"She took up with some other man, Josie."

Lee looked over at me again. I hoped the surprise did not show on my face. I would never want him to think I was judging his mother, or him.

"A traveling man. This fella still had a horse and wagon, where others usually ride the rails now. Ziglar's his name. He told us he liked the freedom the horse and wagon gave him. He could reach the farming families where they lived and carry his goods to them."

I thought of the traveling man who came to Winterset. He put word out that he was coming to town by train, and anyone who wanted anything could come see him at the Grange Hall. He worked in concert with the railroads giving farming and crop information sponsored by those companies. He carried samples of goods for men, women, and even children, but we had to wait on anything we ordered through him to come to us by the post.

"We used to look forward to his visits," Lee went on. "He would park out by the barn for a couple of days, to rest his horses, he said. Mr. Ziglar had these iron samples of appliances he was selling. They were heavy, but they were child-size. You know what I'm talking about, don't you, Josie? They had the tiniest detail on them to show how something worked. He always left us kids with one or two of those each year."

I nodded my head. We had a few of those at Mama and Papa's, too.

"I love the little stove with the opening doors. Kenny always plays with the automobile with its wheels that turn."

"Yes. I knew you'd know what I was talking about. That automobile was always my favorite, until Billy got his hands on it and broke the darn wheels."

We laughed for a moment, and then Lee continued.

"At first, Dad was really worried. He wrote a letter to your mother, but she wrote back and said she hadn't heard anything. So then he got mad. I think he put two and two together. Ziglar had been at the farm and was leaving that day. That was the day Mom left us. Dad told us that we were never to speak Mr. Ziglar's name again. 'That man's name' is how he put it.

"I heard him yelling in the barn one time, but he saw me and stopped. He started coughing like I wouldn't know the difference between yelling and coughing.

"Dad just got quiet after that. Quiet and sad. His eyes were empty. He didn't eat much of anything. His clothes started to sag on him. Good thing he had braces on or his britches woulda fallen right off him."

Lee turned to me and chuckled a little, but I didn't laugh with him. His story was too sad to laugh at.

"Days turned to months turned to a year. We were all just waiting. I had to get out of there. Dad barely talked. He kept on taking care of the farm, but it's like he left us, too, Josie. He'd tousle the boys' hair and sit to eat with us, and he pretended to listen to our talk about school or what was happening in town, but when we said anything directly to him, he'd be startled and not know how to answer us.

"I had to take over looking out for Billy and Stubb. They were coming to the age where they needed to know how to shake hands properly, and I let them watch me when I shaved. They really relied on me, but after two seasons of ball, I wasn't asked back by either team. I just felt like I had to get away."

I certainly understood that feeling, but I did not tell him that, since my family was happy and intact. I felt a bit selfish in light of his family's sad circumstances.

He continued, "Belle was still home to take care of the little boys and to take care of Dad. She encouraged me to go when a couple of my pals told me about the logging up in Montana. They told me the work would be hard, but the money was good. And you were there, Josie."

I smiled at him and squeezed his hand. He turned his eyes back to the road and got quiet for a little while.

"I just hope she's all right. I don't know why she would have done such a thing. She was so sad about our little Gracie dying, but that was a couple of years ago now, and why would she leave the family? We all have been so sad about losing Gracie. I hope Mom will come home one day."

I hoped so, too.

Lee had written to his family when we left Montana. He said he want-ed to communicate our plans to them so they would know to expect me, and to give them a few days to get used to the idea of our being married.

We drove up in the car and Lee blew the horn. Belle, Uncle Oliver and the boys came out to greet us, but there was something uncertain in their demeanors. They seemed to hold back a little, and I thought it must be because of me.

Then Aunt Lydia stepped out of the house.

She just stood watching us until Lee spotted her. His face changed quickly to wide-eyed, open-mouthed surprise when she came out after the rest of the family to welcome him home. After a moment, when he was stopped in his tracks, he took her up in a great big hug and looked over her head at me. I think he may have been a little embarrassed that he told me all he did, but when he put her back on the ground, I em-braced my aunt as if I never knew she'd been away.

There was a deafening silence. It was full of unspoken questions. Lee just looked at his parents and then at his sister, hoping for answers.

Aunt Lydia finally said to me, "It's good to see you, dear, but we were a bit shocked to read in Lee's letter that you'd been married."

Belle said under her breath, "Speak for yourself, Mother."

Aunt Lydia's mouth opened in a gasp and her gaze dropped to the ground. She had the look of a scolded child. I saw Belle roll her eyes. Uncle Oliver just sucked at his teeth and gazed past the barn over at his fields. He said nothing in his wife's defense.

Lee and I looked at each other and stayed silent. They had the good manners to not say anything else to us except to offer their congratulations.

We rested there with the family, but first thing Monday morning, Lee went into town and took that job with the machinist. With the rest of his logging money, he found us a little house right on the main street in Havelock. We chose to live there because it was close to his new job. Havelock was also a stop on the Rock Island and Pacific Railroad, about halfway between the Winterset and Seward stations on the same line, where our parents lived.

I kept house while Lee was at work all day. Aunt Grace and Aunt Lydia came to visit sometimes. They praised my housekeeping skills and my baking skills when I gave them some samples of my cobblers. It felt right to finally be the lady of my own house, and I was so grateful to Lee for sharing this life with me. Lee was always so happy to see me at the end of his day, but no more happy than I was to see him.

I immediately became in the family way, and it was ten months after we were married that our little Alberta Elsie was born in the hot summertime. Fourth of July gunshots and fireworks went off in the area, heralding her arrival. At 8 1/4 pounds, 19 inches long, she was a big, healthy girl.

Elsie was precious and perfect. She laughed in Lee's arms her very first week. I was so proud of her and happy to see everyone's pleasure when they held her and saw her sweet face.

Our baby was showered with gifts when we took her to visit her Grandma and Grandpa Franklin near Seward when she was five weeks old. She received a rattle box and a top, dresses with crocheted lace and embroidery, and a book.

My sister Ethel sent Elsie her very first pair of shoes along with Mama and my youngest sister, Edith. They included booties and stockings in her gift when they came on the train for a visit when Elsie was six weeks old. Elsie's first picture was taken with her Aunt Edith and her Grandma Mobley.

My baby so cheered my mama, who kept proclaiming that at 53 she was far too young to be a widow. I missed my father so. He had passed away just four months before Elsie was born. I knew he would have loved my little blue-eyed babe.

Despite the fact that the local roads weren't right for automobiles, Lee kept his car. Since he worked in a mechanic's shop, he was able to spend the time necessary to keep the car running and maintained well. His father suggested he trade it in for a reliable horse and buggy, but Lee wanted something that would be easier to drive around town with the baby. The car had a back seat, so we could ride with passengers as well.

We took the car out after dinner one Wednesday evening with another young couple we had met at the Methodist Church. It was October 4, and Elsie was exactly 3 months old that day. Our companions were newlyweds, like us, and expecting their first child. The men sat up front and we women sat in the back seat. I nursed Elsie and her full belly, along with the motion of the car, put my baby right to sleep. I held her in my arms as she slept, and we all were having a fine time, laughing and singing as we rode around town and a little ways into the countryside and back again.

We dropped our friends off at their home, and we pulled up to our house when Elsie suddenly felt very heavy to me. And still. I looked down at her and she seemed peaceful, but then I realized she was not breathing. I cried out and held her up to try and rouse her, but she would not awaken.

I looked at Lee in desperation. He turned off the car and took her from me. He shook her gently and felt her chest. I pleaded with him to do something to help her. Cradling her little body on his arm, he just looked back at me and shook his head. The breath of life moved through her no longer.

Our baby left us.

The world seemed to fade out around me, and all I could see was my baby. I took her out of Lee's arms, wrapped her tightly in her blanket, and wept over her as Lee ushered me into the house. I sat in the nursing chair with her until Lee was able to bring the doctor.

When the doctor left us, shaking his head and unable to give a conclusive cause of death, he said that the mortician would come in the morning to collect her body for burial.

Lee sat with me as I slowly gave our baby her last bath, dipping a soft cloth in warm, soapy water to wash her. I powdered her body one last time. He leaned down to breath in the sweet smell of her head and then handed me her little brush. I ran it through her silky hair and flipped the ends until it curled just so. I pinned a fresh diaper on her and slowly dressed her in the nicest of her new things: stockings, dress, lace, bonnet, booties. We each took turns kissing her long fingers, and then I tucked the rattle in her chubby little hands. Lee swaddled Elsie in the softest of her blankets and put her in my arms.

Lee turned out the lights and we lay down with our little one between us. This night, she would not wake us with her crying to be fed and changed. This night, we were the ones crying, and neither of us slept a wink.

At the church on Friday, the minister said a few words and we sang a few hymns. We then took our baby to the cemetery up the road from Lee's parents' place. Uncle Oliver had bought a plot for the family, and Elsie was the first to be laid to rest there.

My world stopped. I couldn't catch my breath. I felt like I was falling, but there was no bottom to my descent. I held tight to Lee's strong hand. It was the only thing that could steady me and keep me on the planet.

I have no memory of how we got back to the house. Some people had been by and left food for us in the kitchen, Lee told me later, but I didn't see it as I went into our bedroom.

Aunt Lydia followed me in and silently helped me undress and put on a fresh nightie. She brushed out my long hair, tucked me into bed, and shut the door behind her as she left me alone to cry myself to sleep even though it was the middle of the day.

When I awoke, Lee was next to me, and it was night. His heavy breathing told me he was asleep. I turned over to cuddle into him, and he wrapped his arms around me. He didn't waken but held me close all night. I was comforted, but it didn't seal the gaping chasm in my heart.

I felt so alone without my baby. What was I supposed to do now?

Aunt Lydia stayed for a week, and she made sure I ate something each day. She also made sure I was left alone when all I wanted to do was stay in bed and sleep. She came in to check on me one time, and I was lying looking at the ceiling, tears streaming down my face into a big, wet circle on the pillow. She sat on the bed next to me and took my hand in hers, saying simply, "I know."

And I knew she did. I remembered when she lost her babies. Aunt Grace told me more about it when I first moved here and had wondered aloud if Aunt Lydia was so somber because she disapproved of me.

"No, dearie. You mustn't think a thing of your Aunt Lydia's sternness. She's had some deep heartache and some disappointments in life. She lives with her pain like a fresh wound. She feels deeply, even if it seems like she don't."

I was relieved, but then I wondered what her heartaches and disappointments were. Aunt Grace told me how hard Aunt Lydia grieved after each of her little girls died, and then how she had run off to find comfort in the arms of another man, although I was never to repeat that to anyone.

I didn't judge my aunt for that. I didn't understand it, but I believed that unless I walked in her shoes I couldn't judge.

And now I appreciated the loving care she was giving me, and her understanding when I just could not drag myself out of bed and get dressed.

Thankfully, I had our little Oliver Thomas, whom we named for our fathers, before Christmas the next year. He was the sunshine in my life, and in Lee's as well. A big personality, Thomas thought he ran the show from the time he was able to exert his influence, which was immediately. He made it clear when he was hungry, and when I fed him, I was rewarded immediately with a huge smile, which just melted my heart and filled in the jagged edges left there when little Elsie died in my arms.

After Tom, we had Cynthia Luella, who was also very headstrong. She was dainty with huge blue eyes that saw everything and a head full of dark curly hair from the moment she was born. She always wanted her mama, which was flattering, when it wasn't inconvenient.

Lydia Bethalee was our last baby. I wasn't sure I could have children anymore, as I hadn't had my monthly episode since Luella was born. Bethalee was a pleasant surprise. She was tough and feminine at the same time. Her chubby legs pumped hard to keep up with her big brother. She followed him around like a shadow, unless Lee was home, and then her Daddy was her center of gravity. We were so happy to have our family, just as we had dreamed about.

Oregon called to us, and when Lee got a job offer at a major manufacturing company in Vancouver, Washington, right across the river from Oregon, we leaped at the opportunity. Our parents had a hard time letting us go, but we were adults with our own family, so there wasn't much they could say.

My only regret was leaving behind our little Elsie, but I had a little book of memories of her that I made and kept close to me always. She lived on in my heart.

Lee got work immediately upon our arrival in Portland. He took the letter of recommendation his boss in Havelock wrote for him into an automotive shop close to our home that needed a mechanic. He was hired on the spot.

After some years, the Buick Dealership brought him in to manage their shop.

It was early in 1942, when Kaiser Industries opened a shipyard just across the river in Vancouver, Washington, that a friend of a friend got Lee to leave Buick to come run the yards there. He oversaw the construction of Liberty ships and Victory ships and other service ships for the U.S. Navy. His work ethic and productivity drew the attention of Edgar Kaiser, who was the general manager of all the shipyards including two others in Portland, and three more in Richmond, California.

Once the war ended, they had a hard time shifting wartime production to peace-time manufacturing. Kaiser Industries closed the shipyards, but Edgar Kaiser kept Lee on as an employee, eventually bringing him into in his father's Kaiser-Frazer Corporation, which produced cars.

We moved to Michigan the year Edgar became the General Manager of Kaiser-Frazer so Lee could work at the Willow Run plant. Lee was so excited about working with the design team on the Kaiser-Frazer cars that I didn't mind leaving our children and grandchildren for a time.

We didn't have to wait very long to be with them again as Luella and Roy divorced at the end of the year and she brought Linda, who was six, and Diane, who was two, to come stay with us. That made it less lonely when Lee was working long hours.

One day, Lee and I were out running errands, when we were hit broadside. Our car was crushed. I was flung into the back seat, and somehow during the collision, Lee's leg got caught up in the steering wheel and he suffered a compound fracture. The other engineers at Willow Run said we were very lucky to have survived the crash. We both wound up in the hospital for a few days. I was just bruised up and got to go home first, but Lee had to have surgery to put his leg back together. Even after his recovery, he always had a limp.

I was so proud of Lee. In spite of the time he had to take off to recover, his long hours at the plant resulted in his promotion to head up the experimental department, which he had already created.

To demonstrate his car's fuel efficiency, as a consultant engineer, Lee drove the Henry J Corsair on the Mobilegas Economy Run for Kaiser-Frazer. Most of the major car producers entered cars into this annual rally out of Los Angeles.

I longed to join him, but women were not allowed to participate yet. Lee and Willard McArthy, who was the driver, were joined by a United States Auto Club observer to make sure they conducted themselves according to Hoyle on the road. They drove from Los Angeles to Sun Valley via the Grand Canyon and Salt Lake City in three days, winning the whole competition on fuel efficiency.

The Kaiser-Fraser cars seemed so promising, and we were all so disappointed when the company phased out of automobile production in spite of the good results from the annual road trip contests, but I was very happy to go back home to Portland.

Lee was grateful to have been employed by the Kaiser Company, and I thought how thrilled he would have been that Nancy did her nursing education to become a Registered Nurse at Kaiser Foundation School of Nursing in Oakland, California.

When she was still in high school, Nancy wrote to us about her driving course. Lee and I both had vivid memories of our accident in 1950 when we still lived in Michigan. Lee became much more vigilant as a defensive driver, and we never had another accident. He wanted to instill crucial driving precautions and practices in our children and grandchildren. It may have been too late for our children, but Lee took the opportunity to share what he knew with his granddaughter.

Lee came home to the letter from our Nancy. He had sat right down to respond to her, and I peeked at what he left on his correspondence pad when he went in to take his bath after he concluded the letter.

Portland Oregon
Nov 11, 1958

Dearest Nancy - Just a note in answer to your letter which we were so glad to get. Besides it has been a long time since I have had a love letter from a beautiful young lady. Why do you have to grow up so fast? It is not such a very long time since you was our baby, remember?

I think it is fine that you are taking the driving course in school. I am sure you will be starting to drive with a great deal more knowledge, and respect for wisdom of observing all of the fundamental safety rules than those who start to drive without the training. I don't imagine I can tell you anything which they don't have in the course, but I will mention a few things which no doubt will be repetitious but some things related to driving safety cannot be repeated too often.

#1 Always remember the car you are driving can be an instrument of death. You as the driver are responsible.
#2 Never take your eyes off the road while the car is moving.
#3 Never let conversation by others distract you from the business at hand.
#4 Your state law may say the car on the right has the right away but if there is any doubt, give it to the car on the left. It may save yours and other lives.
#5 Be sure you stay far enough behind the car ahead so that you can stop with space to spare in any emergency.
#6 Never drive a car with windshield, back light, or windows that are frosty, fogged, or dirty. Stop and clean them off.
#7 Be sure the following safety items on your car are in good working condition. Brakes, steering, all lights, horns, windshield wipers, tires, and engine. If any one of these are faulty, an accident can result.
#8 Above all, practice courtesy and respect for other drivers, and remember you are only one of millions who share the same privileges on the highways and streets.

Good luck, Honey, and God be with you.
We will be seeing you 11-19-58 - 7:55PM TWA Flight 212
Much Love, Grandpa

I found an envelope in his drawer and put a 3-cent liberty stamp and a 4-cent Lincoln stamp in the upper right corner. Lee had a self-inking address stamper with *"A. L. Franklin"* and our address, *"2341 S. E. 53rd Portland, Oregon"*. I pushed the stamper down onto the upper left corner of the front of the envelope to leave an imprint, and then onto the flap on the back of the envelope, where it left a clearer imprint. I set it on top of his letter with the red pen he had used to write the letter so he could address it in the same ink.

When I put it out for the mailman to take in the morning, I could see that Lee had written *"Air Mail"* across the top and then addressed it to *"Miss Nancy Ellstrom 5701 Calle Del Paisano Phoenix, Arizona"*

The sun rose slowly, illuminating the kitchen where I lay on the cold linoleum floor after a painful, lonely night. The light was faint at first, and everything I could see, the table legs and chair legs, and ironing board were various shades of gray.

Usually at this time, I'd be up after a comfortable night in bed, letting Josephine out into the backyard to hunt for her breakfast while I got mine.

On the kitchen table, I kept a little wooden box full of pastel-colored scripture scrolls. Before I ate each morning, I picked out a scripture for the day with the wooden picker that just fit into the rolled-up papers and allowed me to pull one out. I took the tiny paper ring off and unrolled the paper, revealing my Word of God for the day.

Yesterday's was from Jeremiah, my favorite book. *"For I know the plans I have for you,' declares the Lord, 'plans to prosper you and not to harm you, plans to give you a hope and a future.'Jeremiah 29:11."* I ran that through my head all night to try to reassure myself that it was not an accident, and that God was with me.

I ate the same breakfast each morning: a soft-boiled egg and buttered white bread toast with marmalade, usually accompanied by a cup of coffee with cream that I savored over the daily crossword from the newspaper that landed on my front doorstep around 4 'o clock every morning.

I had heard the thud as it landed this particular morning. I'm sure my little house looked the same as it always did: dark with the blinds drawn, for I was not one to rise before the paper arrived.

Bethalee, on the other hand, was always up at three or three-thirty when she visited, ready to dive into the puzzle as soon as it came. She brought me gifts of fresh crossword books, so she could have the challenge of the newspaper puzzle. I never told her the book puzzles were not nearly as enjoyable for me, but once I got used to them, they were entertaining as well.

Luella kept me supplied with the puzzle books lest I run out of things to do, and I also continued to solve the daily newspaper puzzle when Bethalee was not visiting.

I cringed at the memory of her recent trip and my embarrassing lapse the morning I came out from my bedroom looking forward to spending a day with my visiting daughter, only to be greeted by a strange man sitting at my kitchen table.

He wore a brown cardigan sweater over a turtleneck, and when he rose to greet me, he called me "mother". His whiskers scratched my cheek, and I didn't recognize his bald head. He had put his cigarette in the ashtray but picked it up when he took his seat again. I felt confused and confessed, "I think I'm supposed to know you, aren't I?"

He laughed and said, "I hope so. I've been sleeping with your daughter for 10 years now."

"It's Howard, Mother. You know Howard," Bethalee reminded me as she came into the room behind me from the bathroom. She had just finished getting dressed for the day, her crossword done and her pot of coffee already drunk.

They both laughed, and I was grateful to not feel they were laughing at my expense. It felt like they were laughing with me, so I caught the giggles myself.

Luella and Roy came home from BINGO at the usual time but abandoned their routine of checking on me. A teary-eyed, remorseful Luella would tell me late the next morning that she thought I was already in bed asleep since all my lights were out. They didn't hear me call out to them.

It was a long night. I was cold. I was frightened. I wished I was not alone. I missed my Lee more that night than I had in a good long time, but I also felt like he was close by. Even though I couldn't see him, it was like he was there with me, sitting next to me on the floor, holding my hand, stroking my hair, because that's what he used to do when I was ill or in pain. He tried to make me laugh.

Lying on the floor, I tried to imagine how he might make me laugh in this circumstance, and I didn't know. It had been too long since he had done it—17 years since Lee had left us in 1959. Or maybe at the age of 95, just two months shy of 96, my brain just couldn't remember anything anymore.

No, that wasn't true. I may not have been able to remember my daughter Bethalee's new husband's name, but I could remember everything about Lee. He had a special way that I just couldn't imitate. I could hear as clearly as if he were saying it in my ear, his warm baritone speaking my name, "Josie."

Roy called for the ambulance, and it arrived to take me down the road to the hospital, where I was admitted and given a welcome dose of morphine to ease my pain. The young paramedics were so kind, and as gentle as could be with me, covering me with a warm blanket and lifting me on a stretcher that they carried in their strong hands to the ambulance.

Luella followed behind, shoving my book of crossword puzzles and a pen into my handbag. "You'll need something to occupy your mind in the hospital, Momma." She called back to Roy to mop up the floor where I had left the puddle in the middle of the night.

"And lock up before you come along to the hospital," she added.

"Yes, Mother," he replied obediently.

Luella climbed in next to me and held my hand as we drove through the city. Sirens wailed out loud for everyone to hear the deep, quiet despair I felt in my humiliation, in my physical brokenness, in my helplessness, in my fear.

HOW THE PRODIGAL IS MET

Terrified and exhilarated, I rode silently into town next to Mr. Ziglar. When we approached the turn to head into the town center, I slipped into the back of the wagon so no one would see me. My companion seemed to understand why I did this without my having to explain myself.

He brought the horses to a stop, rested the reins on the buckboard, and set the brake.

"I'll come back from the mercantile shortly, and then we'll be on our way. Might you be needin' anything?"

There was that question that he asked me when we first met. I shook my head at him lest my voice carry to an ear that would recognize it and start the gossip while I was still around to hear it.

When he returned, Mr. Ziglar climbed up onto the wagon seat after untying his team. He turned back to look at me and quietly asked me again, "You sure, Mrs. Franklin? I can take you back home now. Your cows are gonna need some attendin' to soon."

I just looked at him. In his face, I saw the means of escape from the drudgery of my life. I saw adventure. I saw freedom. I was not about to leave the wagon.

He turned around and just sat for a moment facing the horses' backsides. I saw his shoulders rise and fall as he took in a deep breath and exhaled slowly. He shifted around in his seat and took in my face with his dark, searching eyes. I feared he'd gathered the courage to kick me out of his rig and send me packing. It occurred to me that he may not want me after all.

"Well, I guess you better call me Isaac then, Lydia."

His eyes held mine for a moment, and then they fell to my lips, and I felt a blush rise to redden my face. He smiled, winked at me, and turned back to his Morgans.

Mr. Ziglar was whistling a saucy ragtime tune as he drove the horses out of town heading south toward Kansas.

On the road, Isaac Ziglar was different.

At my kitchen table, he had told me funny stories about his customers. He had complimented me, "Your pies are the most delicious in the county, Mrs. Franklin."

He told me, "You sure are a sight for sore eyes, Mrs. Franklin."

He recited poetry to me that made my stomach get all fluttery until my knees nearly gave out on me.

That Mr. Ziglar existed only at my kitchen table.

The Mr. Ziglar that rode from community to community was quiet and did not take the time to talk to me about much of anyone or anything. His well of sweet poems seemed to have dried up overnight. He had no more compliments or kind words for me.

He was stuck with me. I know he felt that way when he would walk fast in front of me when we went into towns. He presented me in obligatory introductions usually as an afterthought—by my first name, since calling me Mrs. Franklin would have raised some eyebrows and made people question us.

Taking another man's wife around with him, and sleeping with her in the same bed, would have been met with much disapproval for sure. We did not explain ourselves, and then we saw that people believed we were married and just assumed we should be traveling around in this little wagon together.

In spite of all that, he did not want to appear to be a man with no integrity. There were enough stories about lying, cheating, stealing traveling men. He already had to contend with that reputation so he could make an honest living filling the household needs of his customers.

Mr. Ziglar lost all consideration for me. Now I was just a burden to him. When he just wanted his books around him, I was forced to move them myself, despite his annoyance, to make room for me to sleep alongside him.

After a while, he took to belching and passing gas freely right next to me as if he was all alone, flapping the blanket when we were in bed, or leaning over to lift the butt cheek closest to me on that wagon seat. He made no apologies and never bothered to ask me to excuse him. I had the feeling that complaining about it would bring no change, so I just held my nose and refused to talk to him for a time, not that he was seeking me out for conversation. I considered returning fire with fire, but I chose to maintain my dignity instead.

After a time, Isaac wasn't even interested in the physical closeness that was so passionate in the beginning. Our first night together, we were both so enthusiastic that I had some clothes to mend the next day. The second night when he put his hands on me, something tugged at my memory. My husband seemed to be there with us. Disapproving. Hurt. So hurt by what I was doing. I started to cry. Isaac did not like that one bit, so he shushed me and turned his back on me. He was soon snoring, and I cried myself to sleep.

In all our years together, Oliver never bothered to figure out how to make my body feel the amazing things Isaac did from the very first time we were together. Oliver may not have been skilled as a lover, but he loved me in his way, and then he held me close. I had made my decision, however. I was a state away, and I could not return now. I had fallen into sin. I had left my marriage and my children for a man I thought I knew, a man I thought wanted me as much as I thought I wanted him.

I was so wrong. My perception was so wrong. I did not know what I had been so sure of. It made me uncertain about myself in a way I had never felt before. I thought I was secure in who I was and what I knew. I was not. I was blind. I made a huge mistake. I felt so stupid.

Surely, I'd fallen so far that heaven would not be an option for me now. I wept when I allowed myself to consider that I would not see my girls who had gone before me, without sin and now secure in the arms of Jesus.

Or was that true? I believed it so certainly, and now I realized I may be wrong about everything, even about my understanding of heaven and hell. Our ongoing journey from town to town, and from farm to farm, gave me much time to ponder. I was never able to get any clear answer, though.

Every day for two years, I wanted to draw Isaac out so he would treat me like he always had during his yearly visits to our farm to supply us with hardware and dried goods, when he would charm the children and woo me with his poems and stories of fantasy and adventure. He had even put Oliver under his spell, talking about the weather and crops in different parts of the country. Oliver got some ideas from him about how to grow to the greatest results and harvest the most corn of highest quality. Oliver was so proud of his corn crops.

I think we all had been seduced by Mr. Ziglar, but now I knew the real Isaac Ziglar. He was a quiet man who remembered, once I was a constant companion for him, that he needed his solitude. I believe he knew it all along, but perhaps the novelty of having a woman join him had seemed enticing. The reality of my presence overwhelmed him. He felt no qualms about having taken the wife of another man. He wasn't concerned about heaven or hell. He only believed that each day is a new day. If on this day a woman chose to be with him, he'd let her come along. On that same day, the woman's husband could choose to be hurt or angry or upset, or not. Isaac did not believe he was responsible for how that other man chose to feel.

Isaac talked about choice often. "We are each born with free will," he would say.

"God gave us that gift of choice. Choice about actions, and choice about how we feel and react to what we do or to what others do to us. It's none of my business how anyone might feel about me or judge me."

It made sense in my head, but I just couldn't feel it in my heart, so I prayed for his soul. I prayed for my own soul as well.

It was just another day. Not a cloud in the sky, and the faintest of breezes blowing wisps of hair about my face as the horses trotted out of the little town where we had spent the past week.

"Lydia, you know how I believe in free will and choice, don't you?"

I nodded.

"Well, I choose for you not to be with me anymore. Where should I drop you off?"

His voice was so cold, his tone so flat.

"No, Isaac. I would like to continue with you."

"Staying with me is not an option for you, Lydia."

I was dumbstruck, and I chose not to respond to him right then. In fact, I stayed silent for a few days.

Finally, Isaac said, "Lydia, your silence is even worse than your talking. You have to leave me now. Where am I taking you?"

Isaac was very matter of fact. His tone reminded me of Pa when he had made up his mind and there would be no more discussion on the matter. I realized my time with him was done.

"Where are we?"

"Iowa."

"Then you will take me to my sister's in Winterset."

Isaac encouraged the horses to go faster. He could not wait to get me to my sister's, to leave me there and go on without me. Isaac enjoyed my presence oh, for about a day, and then he did not. He wanted his solitude back. He wanted to not share his small wagon space with me anymore. He was tired of having me with him constantly. He said as much to me.

"Do you ever shut up, Lydia?"

I felt like I barely spoke because I sensed his need for peace. I knew he had been alone for all those years. I had assumed that alone meant lonely. Not for him. He was not lonely, like I would have been. I was used to having people around me all the time: Oliver, the children, my siblings before I had my own family. The quiet was sometimes too much for me. I wanted to hear something. I wanted to have communication. I wanted connection.

I was with Isaac constantly for two years, just like I had fantasized about, and just like I thought I wanted. I never felt lonelier in all my life.

We didn't speak again until after we crossed into Madison County, when I had to give him directions. Pillows of bright white clouds floated in the blue sky. Long dirt roads passed by old familiar places. The rhythmic clip-clopping of the horses' hooves echoed around us as we passed through a covered wooden bridge toward Dutch's home. The river burbled below, and the soft lowing of a cow greeted us. These sounds used to seem romantic and beautiful to me, when Oliver brought me to the bridges. Now they were just a witness to my shame; I was about to appear with a man to whom I was not married.

It had been two years since I had seen my own family. About four since I had seen my sister. I hadn't allowed myself the luxury of missing any of them too much. I had left them, so I did not feel that I deserved to miss them. Although I felt so lonely with Isaac, I had not thought of going home again. I simply could not imagine having to face those I had left.

Now Isaac gave me no choice. I had no other place to go.

Had they missed me? What did Dutch know about where I had been? About what I had done? Even though I felt closer to my sister, Grace, since we had all move to Nebraska, I always knew Amy and Dutch could see me most clearly. Dutch was very attentive when I was a child, but Amy, who had also lost a child, understood me in a way Dutch never could. They, above all my other sisters, knew me best. I don't know how or why, but for some reason, I knew that Dutch loved me best.

Pa had been gone for a few years, I realized. He had died just before my little girl, Gracie, had died. It had been a comfort at the time, knowing that Pa was there to welcome our Gracie into heaven, but my mama had been left alone. I knew that she was staying with Hi and Dora when I left, but I had no idea where she was now, since I had not written to anyone from the road.

There had not really been time. We were always on the move, and Isaac expected me to help him keep his rig neat and make sure his inventory was clean and ready to be sold. He expected me to cook when we were on the open road. Occasionally, we would eat with our customers, and some even put us up in their barns if there was a storm.

When we were in towns, he would splurge on a room at an inn, and we'd get baths and a soft bed to share. Isaac's mood always picked up, and he usually felt amorous on those nights. After finally falling asleep, he wouldn't wake up until eight or so, and then he wanted to be frisky with me again before we got out of bed. I liked that. There was never time for that on the farm, and the children's presence had always kept Oliver and me from taking our time in the morning.

Although, I did remember the rare few times when all the children were gone to school or off with my sisters' families, when Oliver would come in from the fields for lunch and we'd have dessert in the bedroom. Those were happier times, when my heart was not so heavy, and we could laugh together. We had not laughed together in so long.

Isaac was so somber on the road; I could count the times we laughed on both hands. It was usually in the hotel rooms where we stayed. I felt worldly in those hotel rooms, and like a big-city girl. Isaac taught me new things about how to use my body, and how a man could use his body, and how bodies could be used together to provide pleasure for themselves and for each other in ways I'd never dreamed of before. I was daring, even brazen, exposing myself to Isaac in ways I never could with Oliver, even though we had been together for over two decades. Oliver's modesty had made me feel uncomfortable being immodest in his presence, as if my shamelessness was a shameful thing even with my own husband.

No one realized that Isaac and I were not a married couple, and an adventurous part of me reveled in having such liberation, and in the danger of having such a secret.

My stomach always churned at check-in, for fear they would sniff out the truth. We could be found out at any time, but we never were. I relaxed when we had the room all to ourselves, but in public, I carried the burden of our lie with me every single day. I would no longer have to lie about our relationship, for we would not be together anymore. For a brief moment, a wave of warm relief washed over me.

As we went down the road I remembered so well from years of walking along it to get to my sister's home, I recognized familiar land-marks. The neighbor's faded barn, the stone well, the gnarled tree, the still-broken fence, the curves and dips in the road, the softly tinkling stream.

Then I saw it. Dutch's house stood as it always had, and there she was, my older sister, kneeling in her garden.

I could tell she heard us when she looked up, and when she could not quite make us out, she stood up to see who was coming. Something in her stance softened when she saw me, and even though I was over-come with the emotion of seeing her again, I could not wave or even smile. My mortification was too much for me. I was with this man whom I had run away with, only to be dropped off in humiliation.

The horses came to an abrupt halt in front of Dutch and Tom's house, and Isaac reached behind him to lift up the bag he'd made sure I packed that morning. He held it out in front of me. After two years of anchoring myself to him, he was cutting me loose, and I felt suddenly adrift. I searched his face; for what, I don't know. He did not return my look but held his eyes steady on the ground where it seemed he wanted me to be standing. I sighed and rose from the seat. I backed myself down, unaided, to the spot his gaze directed me to.

His demeanor showed how done he was with me and our journey together. He could not even bring himself to look at me, and he had no goodbye for me, nor would he hear mine for him, had I one to give him. I did not introduce him to my sister. It struck me that he did not deserve to make her acquaintance.

I was not choosing this, and so I resented him for taking this adventure away from me. I hated him for not loving me, especially after everything we had done so intimately together. It lifted some of my distress when it suddenly occurred to me then that I did not actually love him. I never had.

He had not taken advantage of me. We had used each other. We had been together for selfish reasons, seeking to fill voids in our hearts, seeking to amuse ourselves, seeking to escape the drudgery of our routines, seeking to satisfy our unsated, carnal, lustful urges like animals. But nothing more. There was nothing tender or loving about our relationship.

Looking up at his face, I could see him in a fresh light. He was a stranger to me. This was someone I thought I used to know, someone I thought I cared about, but no longer. And he was wholly unattractive. He was paunchy and lacking in the kind of physical strength that always appealed to me, the kind that came from working hard, like Oliver did. This man just sat behind horses all day long. I could not recall what I ever saw in him.

When he dropped my bag to the earth next to me, Dutch moved to stand behind me. Without a word to either of us, he called out to the horses and made them pull away so quickly, it seemed the wagon wheels would run right over me. Dutch grabbed my shoulders and pulled me back toward her. She put her arm around my shoulders and held my near hand with her other hand, cradling me.

Her embrace was comforting, yet I felt smothered at the same time. I knew that she could sense my humiliation. The tension between Isaac and me was obvious.

I shifted my eyes away from the departing wagon and scanned the green-leafed and golden-tasseled horizon before us. I breathed in deeply, shook my head a little, and pulled away from my sister, shrugging my shoulders to get her off me. When I finally looked at her, I was determined not to give anything away. I merely said, "Hello Dutch."

"Where have you been, Lydia?" Dutch finally asked after I followed her into the house.

Dutch took my valise from my hands and set it on the bed in the spare room next to the kitchen. She poured a glass of cool clear well water and set it down in front of me. We sat in silence at the kitchen table.

My sister's hands had dirt on them. She'd been pulling the weeds out of the ground so they wouldn't choke the sweet peas that grew tall on the vines she had attached to tall wooden stakes along the length of the rows. The dirt was under her nails, and as we sat there not speaking, she picked at the dirt with the edges of her apron.

I could feel her gaze upon my face, studying me. I looked out the window. Nothing was in my mind but the cold way Isaac had just dismissed me. Dutch must have grown tired of waiting for me to join her because her question was loud enough to jolt me back to the room.

"Where have you been, Lydia?" she asked again.

I felt like a child under her gaze. She wanted to scold me, and she was concerned at the same time.

"Over a year ago, Oliver wrote asking if you'd been in touch with us. I told him you had not. I don't think he asked anyone else. I think he sorted out what happened. What did happen, Lydia?"

"Have you seen him?"

"I went out and visited Grace last year. I saw Oliver and the children, but we didn't speak of you at all. I figured he'd say anything he knew, and he must have figured the same, for it never came up."

I was surprised. And hurt Oliver never went looking for me. Did he not care?

"He didn't come looking for me. He doesn't care about me."

Dutch hit her hand flat on the kitchen table.

"Oh! You and your crazy ideas, Lydia! Doesn't care about you? His letter was frantic. He was very worried. Are you aware that he had crops to put in about the time you left, Lydia? When should he have gone looking for you? Did you even think of your children? They might've been old enough to do chores, but they were not old enough to run a farm alone. When and how was Oliver supposed to go after you?"

"Can I see the letter?"

"No!"

I was about to protest—after all, my husband did write it—but Dutch cut me off.

"I burned it. I didn't want anyone else to witness poor Oliver's humiliation. He's a good man, Lydia. What were you thinking?"

I realized she was right. I felt the heat come up on my face. I kept embarrassing myself; I could not have felt any worse about myself. I must be the most horrid person in the world. I began to cry. Tears streamed down my face, and I nearly choked as my throat tightened. I had a hard time breathing.

"I'm so ashamed, Dutch. What did I do?"

She looked at me in disbelief. She was my mirror of self-ridicule. I felt disgusting.

"Well, you're home now, Lydia."

She got up, left the table, and silently walked out of the room. She stood on the ground just outside the kitchen door and faced her garden. I saw her sigh. A deep breath in, her shoulders rose and fell as she breathed out. And then she stepped to the place she had risen from when she first saw us approach.

I followed Dutch out to the garden, and although I had no apron, I took another row and started pulling weeds. We moved in silence down the rows until we both reached the end. She took the weeds out of my hand and dropped them together with hers on a pile near where we stood. She turned to face me.

My older sister's face was more like Mama's than mine. Her soft, pale skin was clear and the downy hair on her pink cheeks reminded me of ripe peaches. Wisps of her graying, blonde hair had escaped her high bun and framed her light blue eyes that looked at me expectantly. Her thin lips were closed, and the corners of her mouth turned downward, not in a frown, but because that's how all our mouths were made.

Dutch had always been the beauty in the family; there was something noble or regal in her bearing, the way she kept her shoulders back and lifted her chin, holding her head high. I would have to remember to keep my chin up. I wondered if she had any regrets in her life.

"Do you remember that day I spent in the barn, Dutch, when none of you could find me?"

She nodded her head yes.

"I want to go back there."

"Back to the barn?"

"No, back to the place where no one could find me."

"Why?" she asked. Was that annoyance I heard in her tone? I searched her face, but her expression was gentle. She was not going to scold me.

"Because…"

I began to answer, but then words left me. I didn't know how to continue. I didn't know why. I only knew I felt free for a time. Until I wasn't. No obligations, no pressure to get anything done, no responsibilities. It did weigh heavy on me, the fact that I had run away from those responsibilities, from my children; that in two years I never once looked back. I was free. I was young again. I was seeing new places, meeting new people. No one knew me. They couldn't judge me or how I did or didn't do things.

They did not judge me for how I never wept for my baby Gracie when she died. I did weep, just not in public, just not when anyone was home. It was no one's business, my grief. I had to go on. I had to function, and I had no time to fulfill anyone's expectations of how I should be.

Dutch was patient with me. She was quiet while I worked it out in my head.

"Because I didn't want to have to answer to anyone."

"Did it have to do with losing Grace? You didn't mourn for her like you did with the others."

I felt angry then.

"What do you know, Dutch, about my grief? What do you know about losing a child? Nothing. You've not lost a one. I've buried three. Three girls. Please don't ask me questions!"

"Don't ask you questions?" Dutch echoed my words back to me, but now her tone was stern. "You've been gone for two years, Lydia! Oliver didn't know where you were. Mother was so scared for your safety."

"Mother knows?"

"She didn't hear from you, Lydia. I had to tell her why."

"I left a note."

"A note! You gave no information in the note. It just said you were leaving. You gave no time frame, no destination, and no reason! What was your husband supposed to think? What were your children supposed to do without their mother? Your family looked for you to come home every day. And now here you are, a whole state away from them. Why come here, Lydia? Why now?"

"I missed you, Dutch. You were close by, and when Isaac insisted on dropping me off somewhere, I told him to bring me to you."

"Who is this man, Isaac? He seemed unkind. He seemed resentful of you, Lydia. Why would he have those kinds of feelings toward you? You weren't with him the whole time you were gone, were you?"

I didn't have to say a word. After a mere moment of silence, Dutch had the realization. It dawned on her that my relationship with Isaac was more than just casual acquaintances.

"Oh. You were."

She got quiet and just looked at me again, but I covered my face with my hands. How could I tell her what our relationship was? How could I utter the words that I'd been unfaithful to my husband? I felt my face get hot, and I knew it was red. I couldn't face her judgment. I did not want to be judged. I did not want to be forced to feel the shame that was in my heart. But then my sister gave me a moment of mercy.

"Come inside, Lydia. Let's start dinner before the kids get home."

It wasn't long until Dutch's children came home from school, and then Tom came in from his smithy shop in town. They were surprised to see me. They asked me when had I arrived and how had I gotten there and for how long was I staying, and was I coming to the picnic to celebrate Granny Chloe Gold's birthday? I asked them about school, and they told me about their new calf.

I started to feel like myself again. Tom was quiet, as always, and his only contribution to the conversation was something about the corn and how happy Oliver must have been about his crops last year. I did not reply.

Dutch and Tom had chosen to stay in Winterset, along with Clary and Bill, when the rest of us felt the call of the western frontiers, the wide open, relatively virgin land where we could build homes, grow crops, raise families.

"I've done enough moving and building for my lifetime, thanks but no thanks," Tom had said when Oliver brought up the possibility of them joining us.

They were all content to remain behind. When Oliver surprised us with the news that he and I would be leaving our long-time home, I quickly grew as excited about the adventure, even as I was scared and sad to be leaving my childhood home.

I believe Pa would have gone along with us to Nebraska immediately, had Mama allowed it. He did manage to convince her to try it, and a year later they followed us west, renting a place close to town where Mama could have a nice garden and Pa could go off and do odd jobs like cutting sod on the prairie. They eventually ended up back in Iowa. Mama wanted her roots to stay put, for they had done enough moving in their life together, coming all the way from New York by way of Wisconsin and Minnesota, where I'd been born. Clary and Dutch were both close by and were able to look after our Mama after Pa passed into his eternal rest.

Dutch told me that since our oldest sister, Clary, had lost her husband the year after we lost Papa, she was the one Mama stayed with the most. That arrangement worked out well for both of them, especially since Clary was left with the youngest three of their children to bring up on her own. I couldn't imagine being left alone to raise my children. Then I remembered that was just what I did to my husband. Another wave of guilt washed over me.

As I got into bed that night, alone, I realized that although I'd been shocked to be dumped so unceremoniously at my sister's by a man I had tried to make a life with, I did not miss him. The clean, crisp sheets and wide space that enfolded me felt like a baptism, a cleansing and a renewing of my spirit that could only come from leaving one man and returning to my husband.

Oliver was a stranger to me now. I had not spoken with my husband in nearly two years, and all the successes and failures he'd been through in that time were lost on me as I had disconnected myself from our life. But I remembered that it was long before I left that I felt estranged from him even though we shared a bed.

I realized that I missed him. I missed our children. So much can happen in two years on a farm and in the life of a child. Big things, little things. It's the littlest things that matter most, precious moments that have a brief window of time to shine before they pass behind a storm cloud. If we are lucky, they stay crystallized in memory, but sometimes they don't; they just pass along as do the rays of a day's sun, sunrise to sunset, disappearing from view into the darkness of night. Like the face of a loved one. Like the faces of my babies, my little ones who died. Their faces were in my other children's faces. I recognized a shared expression, a similar curve of the cheek or a curl of the hair. These realizations made my living children all the more precious to me.

I had not let myself think about them for two years and now the ache of missing them hit me hard. I cried myself to sleep that night, asking God for forgiveness, asking Him to wash my sins away. The red and blue quilt our Mama had made for Dutch covered me, and I felt the comfort from it as if her arms were around me as I drifted off into a deep, sound sleep.

I sat up with a start in the middle of the night when in a dream, I saw Oliver's mother's face peering down at me. My whole body pulsed with the rapid beat of my heart. Taking in the moonlit room I had been sleeping in, I remembered where I was, and that Mrs. Franklin had died many years ago, so she could not really be there. Breathing a sigh of relief, I lay back down and closed my eyes again, but sleep didn't return right away.

My brain was fully awake again, and I started to hear the inner voice of judgment and criticism that I used against myself. What would Mrs. Franklin think of me? I did regret that I could not be as wonderful a wife for my husband as my father-in-law remembered his first wife, and the mother of his children, to be.

What would Mrs. Franklin make of what I had put her son through? Would she be as forgiving as I was hoping my own mama would be? Would she be patient with me and know just the right words to say to restore my balance and my sense of belonging in the family, which my own choices and actions had undermined for me?

As I drifted off thinking of how my surprise appearance at the family picnic would shock my mama on her special day, I just hoped she would welcome me home.

The morning greeted me as the sun shone through the eastern widow and heated my legs as it rose higher in the sky. I heard the children calling to one another and to their parents. Everyone was bustling about—getting ready to go celebrate our mother and grandmother's birthday. I felt I should get up and help with the preparations and the cooking, but Dutch was letting me sleep in, so I took advantage and lay still for a few more minutes.

What would I say to Mama? She would never speak to me again if she knew the whole truth. I couldn't bear it.

Just then, a sharp rap on the door announced Dutch's entrance into the room to wake me for the day. I greeted her with my question, "What will Mama say?"

Dutch opened the door wider and looked at me still in bed.

"About what?"

Had she already forgiven me? Or did she just not want to talk about it?

"You know about what, sister. I hope she'll be happy to see me again."

"You know she will, Lydia. She is a forgiving woman."

I knew that already, but it was good to hear it from my older sister, who was closer to our mother than anyone else except maybe Clary.

Mama was forgiving, when Dutch pointed out all those years ago that my belly was growing bigger, and it was not simply because I was getting fat from eating too much. Mama saw me with new eyes then. She took in my body, and she also realized that I was in the family way. When her eyes came up to meet mine, she already knew the answer to the question I could see was in her head. And then the confirmation allowed her face to relax a little.

"We'll talk about this in time."

"In time" meant as soon as she told Pa and he had been to talk with Mr. Franklin. Together, they worked out the plan for my life and for Oliver's moving forward, and for our little one who came along a few months later. Our "talk" was the parents letting us know what they planned for us and our nodding our heads in obedient agreement. What choice did we have but to go along? We had no better plan ourselves. Oliver had wanted to go to the next county and elope, but then where would we go? We were too young and dependent to have any other options.

Mama never scolded me, and Pa never said a word; he only quietly did what needed to be done, like go and fetch the doctor from town when the baby was coming. Having watched my mama go through labor eight times herself, Pa did not need to be told when it was time to go.

They welcomed my little James with open arms and hearts, and he was just one more child in the family to love. He spent the first two years of his life doted on by loving grandparents, aunts, and uncles, and playing alongside cousins.

I prayed that my mama's arms and heart would be open for me today.

Tom got their new automobile out of the barn, and the boys helped shine it up. I had never ridden in an automobile, and I felt some fear about going so fast.

The children were excited about hiding me away in the back seat, where I would stay until we got to Mama's and she had greeted them. Then they told me that I should jump out of the car to surprise Mama. I was in no mood to jump.

I believe Mama was overwhelmed when she first realized that she was being surprised and honored. More and more people came, and when I finally did get out of the car, she did not greet me as I had hoped. With hands on her hips, she stood back and said, "Well, aren't you cool as a cucumber, just watching everybody."

"I was waiting for everyone to give you your birthday kisses, Mama."

"Well?" she held her arms open for me, and I embraced her and kissed her soft cheek.

"It's good to see you, Lydia," she kissed my cheek and moved on to the next person who wanted to greet her.

It was her day, and she was not going to be overshadowed by her long-absent daughter, her prodigal daughter.

I felt she must have known exactly what I had done, and I feared her disapproval. Perhaps I'd gone past the bounds of her capacity to forgive. Perhaps she just wanted peace, like Mr. Ziglar did, and I just brought discord. Perhaps I was the weed in her garden.

I stayed in the background for the rest of the day. I didn't want to have any attention directed my way, so I barely spoke unless someone addressed me. I redirected attention to Mama, and no one asked me where I had been.

Maybe they really had not missed me. Maybe they had not noticed I had not been chiming in on the round-robin letters that made their way from household to household updating with the latest news. Perhaps my Belle had filled in the particulars for our family and didn't mention her wayward mother's absence. Oliver had been discreet, only going to Dutch with his concerns. Poor Dutch, saddled with the burden of our secret, my betrayal, my husband's shame. I prayed he would have it in his heart to take me back.

I suddenly wanted to know whether he would. I felt impatient at the laziness of the day, as the men played horseshoes and the women stitched a quilt and the screaming children and barking dogs chased each other around the yard. There was laughter all around. There were presents for Mama. There would have been a cake, but our cousin realized she forgot it at home, and that brought on more laughter.

Everyone brought a different dish to share, and when we all went home, they took the leftovers with them. Nevertheless, I spent most of my time in the kitchen doing dishes, and that felt safe to me, since everyone else was outside enjoying the beautiful day and each other's company. I did not fear my family, but I did not feel like explaining myself and being judged.

My sense of security was shattered when my sister-in-law, Youtha, came into the kitchen carrying an armload of dishes to add to the pile I was scrubbing my way through. I had not seen Youtha since she and Fred, Oliver's brother, came by our place with their four children on their way out of town about 20 years earlier. They were on their way to Arkansas, and Youtha was none too happy about moving there.

Besides being 20 years older, she was faded and puffy, the opposite of what she had been when she and Fred married in 1880. I almost didn't recognize her when she first arrived at Mama's party with her oldest daughter, Bertha, who I definitely did not recognize. Youtha did not greet me or seek me out to talk with me, and I did not go out of my way to talk to her either.

She put the dishes down on the table without a word and just stood looking at me with her hands on her hips.

"Hello, Youtha. My hands are soapy, or I'd give you a proper greeting."

"Don't bother, Lydia. Sure good of you to turn up for your Mama's party."

Her tone was cold and sarcastic. I didn't know how to respond to her.

"Where have you been?"

"Pardon?"

"You heard me," she said flatly. "Where have you been?"

Again, I was at a loss for words. How to explain to her? I remembered that after Youtha had their youngest son, Floyd, Fred had taken up with Jennie, a Swedish woman, in Arkansas. Youtha was desperate to keep Fred away from her and took herself and the children back to

Iowa, hoping he would follow, but he didn't. In fact, he stayed away, living for a time in Missouri, and then he asked Youtha for a divorce a decade or so later. He had written to my Oliver very excited about this new wife of his, Jennie, who he went all the way to Idaho to marry. He had been corresponding with her for nearly 20 years, keeping in touch through letters.

I realized then that she knew what I had done. Recalling the moment they had arrived, Bertha's cold stare at me was the evidence that she also knew that I had left my family, much like Fred had left his. A wave of guilt washed over me, and all I could say was, "I'm sorry Youtha."

"You don't have to apologize to me, Lydia. Fred left me, you didn't. But you did leave Oliver. You did leave your children. Tell me, Lydia, how do you face yourself in the mirror every morning? Why did you do it? What brings you back now?"

I wiped my hands on my apron and turned toward her, but I still couldn't find my voice.

"Why?"

I looked up at her, and her tears were not about me and my family; they were about her own experience of being abandoned, and being disregarded, and being forsaken. Tears welled in my eyes and my heart filled with emotions I couldn't even name. I wanted to embrace her, but when I took a step toward her, she backed away from me and left the room, saying over her shoulder, "No!"

So thankful to be alone once more, I sank into the closest chair and took a moment to cry at the table. I felt so much shame and regret. I had judged Fred so harshly, but I was no better than him. I had done the same to my family.

As I thought about the questions Youtha had asked of me, I wondered, too: *How do I live with myself? Why couldn't I have just stayed put with my family two years ago? What made me think that going off with another man would improve my life any?* The only reason I was coming home now was that Isaac didn't want me around. I had been abandoned, disregarded, and forsaken, just the same as I had done to Oliver and our children.

I stood up, wiping my face and blowing my nose, to turn back to the task at hand. Just then, someone else came into the kitchen carrying more dishes for me to wash. It was a neighbor I didn't know, and other than a polite greeting and thanks, we didn't talk. I was grateful.

When it was finally time to go, I kissed my mama on her soft cheek and whispered, "Happy birthday, Mama. I love you."

"More than tongue can tell," she whispered back. She caught my eyes with hers and squeezed my hand tight before she let it go and turned to Dutch to say goodbye to her.

In the car on the way home, Tom said, "I guess we'll just leave the car out front, so it'll be ready to take you to the train in the morning."

I looked at Dutch.

"Train leaves at 7 a.m.," she said without turning her head to look at me.

"Thank you, Tom. Thank you, Dutch."

My heart was heavy. My reprieve was over. I wanted to stay longer, but I knew I couldn't impose upon Dutch and Tom's hospitality any longer.

I didn't want to be in anyone's way, but when someone loves you, they don't feel like you are imposing on them or a burden to them. I realized that Isaac never loved me when he dropped my bag to the ground and then snapped the reins on the horses' rumps to make them go. He never even looked back.

Dutch had witnessed it all. She had wrapped her arms around me, and I needed to feel free, so I shrugged her off. I didn't want to talk about any of it. I didn't want to feel the shame. I didn't want to be the recipient of any judgment.

I would have to now, regardless. I had to go home to face the music. Much as I dreaded it, I also anticipated it. Like any fearful thing, the more I thought about it, the scarier it got. Then in finally doing it,

I realized it was not as painful as I imagined it would be. I wanted to go back to how it used to be, before I made the decision to run away.

That night as I drifted off to sleep in my sister's spare bed, I realized that although she was stern and asked questions I didn't want to answer, Dutch truly loved me. She didn't feel I was a burden or an imposition to her. She welcomed me, fed me, and let me rest with her family for a couple of days. Then she sent me lovingly on my way, back to my own children, my own husband, my own home.

I had been my own judge and crucifier, not Youtha, not my sister, not even my mother.

SENTIMENTAL JOURNEY

When we moved for Dick's job from Chicago to Phoenix in the autumn of 1955, I got into the habit of waking up early in the morning while it was still cool out. My husband, Dick, and our children, Nancy and Jim, slept in for at least an hour longer than I.

Just before the sun rose in the eastern sky, the light that came into the kitchen window was warm and soft. It became my favorite time of day, when the stillness was only interrupted by the newspaper landing with a thump on the front walkway. Other than the sweet songs of the early birds, the only other indication of life was the crowing of a rooster a few blocks away. Then the rattle of the milk truck and deliveries of the sealed glass bottles being made up and down the block signaled that the rest of the neighborhood was also soon to wake up.

Until my family awoke, I was alone with my first cigarette of the day and a mug of coffee, black like my dad always preferred it. I worked the daily newspaper crossword puzzle alone in the silent house. When I heard Dick get up, rouse the kids, and go into the bathroom, I put the puzzle aside and began to get breakfast ready for them. When they were dressed and ready for the day, my sleepy-eyed family came out to the kitchen for their scrambled eggs, buttered white toast with marmalade, and orange juice.

In Chicago, I would bake our bread in the late afternoons so it would be ready by the time Dick came home for dinner. I also made a cinnamon roll for Jim to enjoy hot out of the oven after school as he sat in the middle of the living room rug watching *Howdy Doody* on the television.

Now that we lived in the Arizona desert, I liked to get my baking done early before the heat of the day got to be too much for me in spite of the air conditioning. As they left for school, I would tell Nancy and Jim if I'd be baking bread that morning.

My son was in eighth grade, and his school let out half an hour before the high school. Jim and the boys who came home with him always ate up one whole loaf. They'd want more, but I sent them outside to terrorize the neighborhood as only adolescent boys know how to do.

Knowing Nancy would be home any time, followed just moments later by her friend, Jerry, I'd take out the loaf I always hid away in the pantry for him. The first time Nancy brought him home with her, he was reserved and polite, eating only half the loaf, using a knife to cut off modest pieces.

"Thank you, Mrs. Ellstrom. This is the best bread I've had all day."

When I let him know, eventually, that I baked the whole loaf just for him, he made no apologies about wolfing it down, tearing it apart with his hands.

Laughing at him, I asked, "Didn't you eat lunch today?" to which he replied, "Yes ma'am."

His family was from Texas, and he had been taught southern manners and an easy drawl. Jerry insisted on calling us "ma'am" and "sir", which Dick appreciated, of course, despite his general hatred of that term from his days serving in the Navy.

"I just haven't had any of your warm fresh-out-of-the-oven homemade bread in so long, Half-tan."

Half-tan was a term of endearment he started to use with me in honor of my freckled complexion. Dick did not appreciate that. He felt it was too familiar, but I didn't mind it at all. Mother had always told me my freckles were angel kisses. Apparently, lots of angels had been kissing me before I was born.

"It was just a week ago, Jerry."

"I know it, ma'am, and I sure did miss it."

He was a good-looking boy: tall, dark, and handsome. Nancy told us that he got really good grades, and although he spent most of his time warming the bench, she went to every football game to cheer on … the team. My daughter was very active at school, and at church as well as with Rainbow Girls at the Masonic Lodge. She had nice friends, and I fondly remembered my carefree high school days as she enjoyed her teen years.

They were just now starting their senior year at Scottsdale High School, but Nancy had known Jerry since their freshman year, when he came into the cafeteria shouting a rebel yell. She didn't like that, but she grew to like him. They dated this past summer, but he broke up with her just before school started. She was heartbroken, but she never let on to him, since they were friends first and foremost.

Any time I needed anything from the market, she was happy to hop in my '55 Chevy Bel Air convertible and drive past Jerry's house, which was on the way to the store, and on the way home from the store. She told me that she honked and waved when he was outside.

My thoughts were interrupted by the timer buzzer. I turned off the oven, and I was just pulling out the last of that week's loaves to cool on the kitchen table when the phone rang.

I got to the phone on the third ring.

"Bess, it's Roy."

I was startled by his voice. Roy had never called us. It was always Luella. I was immediately concerned for my sister.

"Is Luella all right, Roy?"

"It's not her, Bess, she's fine."

My heart sank anyway. I sat down to brace for it.

"What's going on, Roy?"

"It's your dad, Bess. He's gone."

"Yes, Roy, he was due to go home from the hospital today, is what Luella told me."

"No Bess, I mean your father has passed away."

"No!"

Mother and Daddy had just been to Phoenix for a visit in April. He was fine then. A little cough, but he was hearty enough. Luella had called a few days before to let me know Daddy was in the hospital with heart trouble, but they expected him to be going home. I was going to call them later to check on him.

Now it was too late. I would never hear my father's voice again.

"No, Roy."

"I'm sorry, Bess. I hate to be the one to tell you."

Surely, he must be joking. Roy was always goofing around. This must be one of those times. He loved to tell the story of the time he was caught using a different voice than his own.

Roy was a florist, and one day he was alone in the shop. Crouching behind the counter to put a new shipment of vases away, he heard the bell on the door ring announcing someone's arrival. Roy heard someone call out with a guttural, nasal, lispy voice, and he thought it must be his friend, with whom he joked around in that kind of voice. He responded in kind, but when he stood up, he saw that it was not his friend, but a customer who happened to have a speech impediment. Roy was caught between a rock and a hard place because he didn't want the customer to think he was making fun of him. He said the customer seemed so pleased to have found another man with the same speech impediment as he, Roy didn't have the heart to come clean, so he continued to talk in that way with the customer until he paid for his flowers and departed.

"This is not funny, Roy Schilling. Don't be cruel. You stop right now."

"Bess, it's true. I'm not joking now. I'm so sorry. The funeral will be on Monday. Momma is very sad, of course, but she's holding up well. She's a strong lady, but she needs her kids around her now. You'll come, of course?"

I couldn't find my voice to respond to him.

"Tom is coming, Bess. He'll be flying up Sunday from San Francisco. He has to be on the air, so he can't leave until then. Can you hear me, Bess? Are you all right?"

"Yes, Roy. OK. Thank you."

The receiver fell to my lap, and I heard Roy saying goodbye, but I couldn't reply. I couldn't get up to hang up the phone. The connection broke when Roy hung up, and I let the buzzing receiver drop to the floor as I broke into uncontrollable sobs.

I couldn't catch my breath. Eventually, I made my way into my bedroom and shut the door. I was still curled up on my bed clutching a drenched hankie hours later when Nancy knocked on my door.

"Mom? Mom, are you OK? Why was the phone off the hook?"

"Come in," I croaked.

Nancy cracked open the door and saw me still in my housecoat from the morning. I never stayed in my housecoat after everyone had gone for the day. I never knew when a neighbor would come by like Dottie MacKenzie, who loved to drop in unannounced. She never stayed very long, but I wanted to be dressed all the same.

"Mom what's wrong?"

"Your grandpa's dead, honey."

"No, Mom."

"Yes, it's true."

I held my arms out to her, but she said, "I'll be right back."

I heard her speaking to someone. I realized it must be Jerry. The kitchen door shut as she saw him out, and I hoped he was taking his bread home. I just couldn't muster the energy to get up to make sure.

When Dick got home and learned the sad news, he got on the phone to Tom to get the details I hadn't been able to ask Roy for. He told us that Dad never left the hospital. Here we all thought he'd be fine, but then suddenly he was just gone. Although he was a healthy man, moderate in all things, his heart gave out on him. There was nothing that could be done.

Dick and I agreed that the expense of a plane ticket would be too much of a strain on our budget, so he put me on a train that night, assuring me I'd make it in plenty of time for the funeral.

Dick did not travel with me. He had to work, and the kids were in school, so I went alone.

On the train, I felt agitated and anxious. I was not interested in the magazines or the book I brought. I got up and went to the dining car to get a drink with my meal money. I wasn't going to eat anyway.

When the waiter set it down on the table, I realized I'd need another, so I went ahead and ordered it before he left me. I lit a cigarette, which I enjoyed before I downed my second drink. The warmth from the alcohol ran down into my body and then reached out through my arms and legs to my fingers and toes.

I returned to my seat, calmer than before, and settled in for a long ride. I lit another cigarette and stared out the window at the passing cityscape that turned into dusky, fading landscapes as we headed west, chasing the sun, and I thought about my father.

I remembered when he got a telegram one afternoon. It was 1942. February. He let Mother see it, and they shared a silent look before Daddy crumpled it up in his fist, went to his bedroom, and shut the door.

"Your Grandma Lydia is dead."

Mother's voice was flat, but she pulled her hanky out of her apron pocket to blot the tears on her cheeks.

"What?" I couldn't believe it. "When? How?"

"I don't know. Your dad got a telegram just now. He will call the folks in Nebraska later to find out."

My Grandma Lydia was a serious woman. She didn't smile unless Dad said something to amuse her. That was not difficult for him to do. My dad was a very charming man. He and Mother used to sing tunes and tease one another. They laughed often. Our house was always full of laughter when I was a child. When Grandma Lydia came to visit, she was more somber than us, and she never joined in with our gaiety.

I wondered whether Tom and Luella knew yet. They had both moved out of Mother and Daddy's house. My older brother, Tom, was a newspaper reporter then, and he lived on his own in Seattle. My sister, Luella, and her husband, Roy, didn't live that far away. I thought about running over to tell her, but there were no details to tell yet, so I decided to wait for Dad to let us know what he learned. He would call Tom himself.

My normally jovial father always had a hearty appetite for the egg, bacon, buttered toast, black coffee, and orange juice Mother lovingly prepared for him each day, but in the morning at breakfast, he was so quiet, and he sat still, barely touching his food. My mother also didn't say much, but when she had finished her toast, she put her little hand on Dad's larger one.

"We've decided that Dad will get on the next train. He'll just make it in time for her funeral."

"I figure an express train will be faster than driving, especially since it being winter, the roads may be ice or worse, snowed under. Better safe than sorry."

I jumped up and kissed his cheek.

"I'm so sorry about Grandma Lydia, Daddy."

He ran his hand over my curly auburn hair, which Mother had, on a number of occasions, told me looked just like his. I had noticed for myself that his hair was just like his mother's, so mine must also be just like Grandma Lydia's. Dad patted my cheek, then he tweaked my nose, which he told me once was just like his mother's nose. The usual sparkle in his eyes was gone that day, but when he looked at me, he smiled, and I felt his love for me even through his heartache.

He took the train to Nebraska, leaving Mother home to stay with me and to help care for Luella's baby, Linda. Being my grandma's namesake, I thought I'd like to go with Daddy to pay my respects, and also to see family back in Nebraska. In the end, I also stayed home to hold down the fort, since I had to go to work anyway.

"Excuse me. Um, excuse me, please."

I was startled back to awareness of my surroundings by an insistent feminine voice. It was dark outside, and some people had made their seats recline and shut their eyes. I looked up to see a stylishly dressed, neatly coiffed young woman standing by my seat.

"May I sit with you? You see, I am traveling alone, and I was sitting in the next car up, but my seatmate complained about my smoking, and I see by your ashtray that you are smoking, and I thought you may not mind it if I was smoking near you."

I was in no mood to be social right then. I had no interest in mindless chit chat with a stranger, so I didn't speak to her. I just gestured at the seat next to me.

"Oh, thank you. I promise not to be a bother. I'll be trying to go to sleep here in just a few minutes once I get settled in."

I moved my magazine from the seat so she could sit down and put it on the windowsill.

"I see you brought a LIFE magazine. I did, too. Don't you just love the pictures? It really brings things to life right there in my living room. I don't even have to see the thing in person. It's in living color from all the way across the country."

Pulling a cigarette out of its pack, I thought about one time when Grandma Lydia visited us when we were little; she brought a LIFE magazine with her. We were all so excited to see it. Luella and I loved to look at the cartoons. We didn't understand them, but the illustrations amused us. Tom read every word from front to back. I pulled in deeply on the cigarette to make the end glow red.

It was an odd habit. I didn't usually think about it at all, but as I observed myself pulling in air and then blowing out smoke, it seemed kind of pointless. Except that I loved smoking. I enjoyed the smell of it and the warmth of it and the sensation of the cigarette in my hand. I felt like someone other than myself when I was smoking; a movie star perhaps, one definitely more sophisticated than I was. And then it became something that my body seemed to need. It steadied my nerves. When did that happen?

I went back in my mind to my first cigarette. I recalled that I stole one from my big brother, Tom. It was on his dresser, and I took it when he was outside. I'd watched him smoke, so I thought it would be a good idea to try it for myself. I took one puff before I was as sick as a dog. I never told anyone, and I must have forgotten how sick it made me, for obviously I tried it again.

It was when we moved to Baltimore about seven years after Dick came home from the war. He was moving up in a nationwide technology company, and we had to go where they needed him. Things changed for our family. Not just our home location, but our relationship to one another. After the initial excitement of the move to a new home in a distant state wore off, and it sank in that I wasn't going home, for I was home, the homesickness took over.

I felt so blue, I could barely get up in the morning. I didn't like our new home. We lived in a huge apartment complex with lots of neighbors so close that we could hear their conversations through the ugly gray walls, which meant that they could hear ours.

It took some time, but once we got acclimated to the bitter winter weather and started making friends, thanks to the Welcome Wagon and the other wives at Dick's job, I didn't long for home nearly as much.

My outlet was playing bridge with girlfriends during the day. The women I played with smoked, so I took it up as well. It was just natural.

I didn't inhale deeply, and I smoked one to their three, so I didn't feel sick from it. Dick had started smoking in the Navy and didn't quit when he came home, but he was critical when I started taking cigarettes from his pack.

We would play couples bridge in the evenings with Dick's work associates and their wives. I started to enjoy drinking liquor at these events. I had always been social. I enjoyed meeting new people and sought the company of my friends, but since we moved, I was surprised to feel a sense of anxiety when we met with his work associates or clients, or even new neighbors. I wasn't sure why, but the cocktails helped to take the edge off, and I felt more comfortable, like I always had in similar situations back home.

This was another new experience for me because Dick and I never drank when we were young. We were both raised in homes that just didn't have liquor. Even during the day, the bridge hostesses would serve cocktails, and then I started to serve them when Dick and I hosted. It helped me get over my nervousness when I was meeting Dick's bosses' wives and making new friends. They were all drinking, so I wanted to go along. Soon, I started to serve them to Dick when he got home from work, even on nights we didn't play bridge. It became a routine.

Before I knew it, it was part of my every day. I would have a drink with Dick and then I'd start to make dinner with a cocktail in my hand, and then I started drinking with lunch even when I wasn't playing bridge.

I felt relaxed when I drank. It helped me to feel better when I started to have questions and doubts about my relationship with my husband that I would never voice aloud to another human being, not even to my sister or my best friend, Jean. It helped me to forget how our relationship started, how he had attacked me on my father's couch that night. I found myself getting angry sometimes, and then I wouldn't let Dick touch me when we were alone in our bedroom, but when I drank, it was easier to be intimate with him, and he seemed to enjoy me more at those times.

Despite that, he started to get on me about having had too much to drink when he got home at night, so I showed him and numbed myself to his criticisms of me by drinking even more once he got home.

Then I couldn't stop drinking. I could still function and keep the house and put myself together to look more than presentable in public, but sometimes I wouldn't answer the phone for a few days in case it was Mother. I didn't want her to know I was drinking liquor.

One time, when some old friends from home came for a visit, I became self-conscious when I realized that they weren't drinking nearly as much as I was. I was embarrassed when I knocked things over and burned the dinner, and I tried to make excuses. Then I was ashamed because they had no response to my excuses. They only looked at each other. I didn't correspond with my friends anymore. I decided not to be their friend, and I used the fact that we continued to move as an excuse.

"I lost touch with her when we moved."

This was what I said about a few friends who didn't drink like I did.

I started to forget things. Dick would bring up a conversation or an event, and I had no recollection of it even though I knew I had been there because I remembered what I had been drinking. I just didn't remember what happened once the drinks were served.

We moved to Phoenix when Nancy was finishing up middle school, and when Dick started to talk about our next move, I put my foot down and insisted we stay put until she finished high school so she wouldn't have to change schools and try to make new friends again.

Nancy and Jim were always good about sticking together when we moved, first to Baltimore and then to Chicago. They were close enough in age that they were a comfort to one another, but now that she was going to be in high school, it would be different. There was a divide between them now that she was that much older.

I loved living in Phoenix, and so did Dick. We made good friends and still played a lot of bridge, but we were able to get outdoors more and enjoy golf like we had when we were first married. I did try to drink less, but Dick and I were struggling to stay loving to one another.

He was angry. I finally realized that that was just him. He had always been angry, but he pretended very well, and when we were new to each other, I chose to overlook his anger and try to soothe him, especially after he came home from the war. That just wasn't working for either of us anymore.

My reverie was interrupted by a high-pitched whiny voice, and once more I became aware of the rocking motion of the train building up speed along the rails; I felt so sleepy all of a sudden.

"Pall Malls are so much smoother than Du Mauriers or Chesterfields, don't you think? My husband insists on buying those if he wants to appear fancy, but he gets Marlboros or Lucky Strike for every day, so I am stuck smoking those."

I held my cigarette up between my first two fingers to see that the end of it was lit all around, and savoring the sweet smell of freshly lit paper and tobacco, I didn't care what brand it was. I studied the manicure I'd given myself just the day before. It was in acceptable condition for the train ride, but once I got to Mother's in a couple of days, I'd have to freshen it up or redo it for the funeral.

"That's a lovely color on your nails. What is it?"

In response, I blew the smoke out of my mouth up toward the roof, and I looked over at my new seatmate. I was unable to immediately recall the answer to her question and found myself unwilling to try. She needed to immediately fill the awkward silence, so she told me about her own nail color as she extended her hand into plain view, wiggling her fingers.

"I usually use Red Rose, but this morning I just felt like a softer color would be nice on my fingers, so I put on Pink Pearl. If you look at my feet, though, you can see I got a little daring and I used Ruby Red on my toes. See?"

She let her shoe fall off her foot, and she extended her leg so I could see her bold red toenails. She looked at me expectantly.

I suddenly felt so sleepy I could barely keep my eyes open. I looked away from her, took another drag, and stubbed out the fire. Since I had only lit up a couple of minutes before, I took care to not bend the cigarette so I could relight it later. Dick had not given me enough money to buy anymore cigarettes while I was traveling, unless I wanted to skip another meal. I tucked the butt back in the pack along with the book of matches. I didn't want the matches to disappear, for then I'd have to ask the porter for more. I took the warm, green and white quilt Grandma Dutch made for me so many years ago out of my bag, and I pulled it up to cover my body. I put my black, silk sleeping mask on my eyes.

"Good-night," I said, speaking aloud to my seatmate for the first and only time.

"Oh, um. Good-night."

I was unable to drift off to sleep, even with the rocking motion of the train moving along the rails. I hoped my mother was holding up OK. Roy said she was, but she was good at seeming well even when she was not.

Mother left teaching when she got married to Daddy. He had only gone to school through sixth grade, and he did well, but I saw on a few occasions that he wasn't too proud to ask Mother for help with spelling or grammar when he was writing something for work. She taught us to read and write our letters, so when Tom, Luella, and I started going to school, we were already ahead of our classmates. Mother and Daddy were so proud that Luella and I were in the College Preparatory Course at Washington High School.

When Luella married Roy and moved out of the house, Mama got a little lonely. Luella had been a constant companion for her. My sister would pretend she was ill so often to stay home, that she and I both graduated from high school in January of 1940 even though she was a year older than me. I didn't ever stay home from school. I enjoyed learning and being with my friends too much.

My first niece, Linda, was born just ten months after Luella's wedding, and Mother was never so happy as when she was with that little baby girl. Luella brought her around every morning on her way to work. Even if she didn't go to work, and it wasn't too long before she stopped working, Luella would still drop her baby girl off, or ask Mother to pick her up, so she could "get some things done."

As we were growing up, our parents treated us all the same, but I knew that Mother always favored Tom. Her first child, Elsie Alberta, died at just three months old, and Tom came next. I think he helped ease the pain of losing that first baby. Once we were all grown and out of the house, Tom always promised Mother he'd come to visit, but he didn't visit nearly as often as she would have liked. He did write to her, and to me, from far-flung places like Cairo, Egypt, or Singapore, or London, England.

Although Mother would never say she missed him, I knew she did because I missed Tom, too. He was our family celebrity. As a newsman on major news networks up and down the west coast, he got to interview regular folks and local politicians, but he also hob-knobbed with celebrities, and he was on a first-name basis with heads of state around the globe. Tom always had the best stories, with pictures to back them up. My favorite gift he gave me, besides that of his time and attention, was an autographed picture of my favorite movie star—at least he was my favorite after I got the picture.

"Best wishes to Bethalee Franklin from Clark Gable"

Tom was always good about sharing what he was up to with me. He often sent photo postcards from exotic ports of call in Asia, Africa, and Europe. Sometimes it would be pictures of the women, usually blondes, he enjoyed spending time with in these foreign lands. Those who knew him professionally were impressed by his worldly sophistication, but to me, he was just my big brother, Tom.

When we were growing up, Tom was a great older brother. He always protected me. He took me with him around the neighborhood and wouldn't tolerate the older boys picking on me. I was much younger than they were, but for some reason, Tom didn't mind me being around. I tried hard to keep up; to run as fast, climb as high, and throw the ball as far. Maybe he didn't have to watch out for me as much as he did for Luella. Luella didn't like running around and getting dirty, and she would often whine and complain.

"Wait for me!" she'd yell when the gang was half a block away from her.

"Come on, Luella," Tom would call to her, frustration in his voice.

She usually chose to stay home with Mother, but when she wanted to join in, Tom would double check with her, "Are you sure, Chickie? We are going to be crossing that stream and climbing those trees you are scared to fall out of."

Sometimes he could dissuade her, but sometimes her mind was made up. She was going to join us whether we liked it or not. I didn't mind her being there, but then I didn't have to look out for her, either.

When Luella left home to marry Roy Schilling, it was just Mother and Dad and I in the house. We had just graduated from Washington High School, and I started working at the phone company downtown when John Donaldson, or Johnny, as we all called him, and I started dating exclusively. We never went to the same school together, but we met because we had so many friends in common. It was while he was away at college and then after he enlisted in the National Guard, that he realized he felt more than platonic affection for me.

Whenever I had a hootenanny at Mother and Dad's, Johnny always showed up with our friends and joined in. He was a lot of fun. He could play the piano well, and he would regale the group with many funny sailing ditties that he knew. He always brought a drink to share with the gang. It was always a bottle or two of fruit juice from his parent's home. They had many fruit trees, so they would sell some of what they harvested at the market. His mother was always making preserves and juicing the fruit. I especially loved her apple cider.

When he was home at Thanksgiving, Johnny asked me to go to the movies with him. Mild mannered and easy going, he was always game for a laugh, and I was happy to go along.

"What are we going to see?"

"Never you mind," he teased me. "You'll see." Johnny had a gleam in his eye, and I knew he would have me laughing in a minute.

"Two for *Strawberry Blonde* please."

He pushed his money under the box office window partition and withdrew two tickets. As we walked into the lobby, he handed my ticket stub to me. He knew I liked to paste such things in my diary. I tucked it in my handbag for safekeeping.

"I thought this would be a fun show to see with my favorite redhead."

Johnny winked at me and held open the door to the theater so I could enter first.

The theater was crowded with other college students home for the holiday. We waved to some people we knew, and Johnny found us two seats far away from anyone who looked familiar.

Just as we sat down, the lights dimmed, the crowd hushed, and the newsreel began. The grainy film showed images of labor strikes and aftermaths of industrial explosions. The narrator promised a brighter economic future with the retooling of manufacturing to meet the war needs of our allies. Chamberlain, the British Prime Minister, reaffirmed the United Kingdom's strong stance against the Nazis and committed to continue to squeeze Hitler by cutting off his oil resources in the Middle East. Japanese delegates were in Washington to get the United States to ease up on them about their occupation of China. Our soldiers were occupying Iceland for strategic advantage in the North Atlantic, and the first American warship was torpedoed by Nazi U-boats.

I was troubled by what I had seen in the news, but I smiled at Johnny, trying to ease my own anxiety about a coming war and dark days that seemed inescapable. I wondered whether he would have to go to fight for democracy against the scourge of fascism, as some posters I'd seen around town suggested we do.

Johnny returned my smile and picked up my hand to hold in his. I turned back to the screen, expecting to laugh with the cartoon, but it was just a version of three little pigs with a Nazi wolf coming after them. Something about buying war bonds to achieve victory. I felt discouraged. There seemed to be no escaping the clouds of conflict that seemed to be getting more ominous each day.

I was so thankful when the second cartoon was funny. It was really an advertisement for an Oldsmobile. Johnny and I joined in with the rest of the audience on the sing-a-long parts. At the end of the reel, the girl and her boyfriend got married, and then they were boxing each other. I didn't understand that part, but my mood was lifted anyway.

Johnny and I smiled at one another again, and he squeezed my hand. I felt happy with him. As I was turning back to the movie screen, someone caught my eye from further down the row. The seats curved in an arc, so that even though we were in the same row, I didn't have to lean forward to see him.

When he smiled at me, I realized it was Dick Ellstrom. I waved at him with my right hand, and when John looked to see who I was waving at, Dick's expression went blank. He just looked away then without acknowledging Johnny. I thought that was odd of him.

"Do you need anything? Would you like something to drink?"

"No. I'm fine, thanks."

I didn't want Johnny to leave right when the movie was about to start.

Throughout the film, each time James Cagney's ex-convict dentist character saw or talked about the enticing redhead in the film, I felt someone looking at me, but I refused to look Dick's way. I was with Johnny, and besides, I didn't want to miss any of the movie.

When he dropped me off at home later that evening, Johnny held my hand as he walked me to the front door.

"Will you be my steady girl when I am home from college, Beth?"

"Why, yes Johnny."

"Only, you are not going to turn mean on me?"

"No! Why would you think that?"

"Well then, you must give up your free-thinking ways, Bethalee."

I knew then that he was making references to the movie we had just seen, and I played along.

"Do you have a cigarette? And a light?"

We laughed at our silliness. It was so easy to be with Johnny. I liked his looks; he was tall and lean with dark hair. He had a strong jawline and in profile, I thought he looked like a movie star. When I saw Montgomery Clift on the big screen for the first time, the resemblance to Johnny was so striking that he took my breath away.

Johnny fastened something on my coat lapel.

"What is this?" I could see a crest and some initials, but I didn't know what it all represented.

"It's my fraternity pin. When a girl agrees to go steady, we give her our pin."

"Oh, I see. Thank you, Johnny. I'm sure it's lovely."

I didn't really see, but I liked it, so I gave him a kiss on the cheek and went into the house. I peeked out at him as I shut the door behind me, and Johnny's face was a wide grin. He jumped off the porch, touching his heels together like we had just seen James Cagney's character do on the big silver screen. I giggled aloud at the sight of him.

Mother and Dad were sitting in the living room listening to the radio. The variety show was on. Dad was tossing a ball from hand to hand as he listened and laughed. Mother was doing a crossword puzzle with her pen going back and forth between clues and spaces, filling most in right away, only skipping the few she didn't know until she was able to fill in the rest and figure it out, or remember the correct word. I started to do them with her, and I realized that the more I did it, the easier it became.

The obscure words or abbreviations became familiar, and in time, I was able to fill in blanks nearly as quickly as my mother could.

They both looked up at me. My dad smiled and tossed the ball my way.

"Hey, kid."

I caught the ball and gently threw it back to him. Mother was looking at me over the tops of her glasses and smiled as she asked, "Did you have fun? How was the show?"

"I did enjoy myself. Johnny pinned me." I held out my lapel so they could see my new accessory.

"One of my pupils used to tell me, 'a pin's a-tickin' me,'" Mother remembered. "His clothes were so ragged, that his mother would pin them together. I guess she couldn't afford the thread to mend them properly."

"A pin's a-tickin' me, Teacher," Dad teased with a falsetto voice and a wink.

"Oh, Lee!" my mother protested, barely concealing a smile.

"Oh, Josie!" my father mimicked her with a gleam in his eye.

"I guess it means that we're going steady."

"Is he one of the boys that used to come to your get-togethers here at the house when you were in school?"

"Yes, Mother. You know him. He's the tall boy with dark hair. He brings bottles of fruit juices from his mother to share with the group."

"Of course. I remember him. Nice boy. Good manners," she replied. "Isn't his father from Scotland?"

I nodded.

"I know that one," Dad said. "Firm handshake, respectful. He's OK with me."

I was happy to have my father's stamp of approval.

"Night, Daddy. Night, Mother. I'm going to bed now. I have to be at work in the morning."

I leaned over to kiss my father's cheek, and he said, "Don't let the bed bugs bite."

I shook my head and turned to kiss Mother's cheek.

"All right, dearie. Love you more than tongue can tell." Mother squeezed my hand as I left them to go into my room.

"Arriving at Union Station in 30 minutes."

I didn't have to take off my mask to know that it was still dark out when the conductor came through announcing our approach into Los Angeles. According to the train schedule, sunrise would not be for another hour after my arrival there.

I had awakened a few hours before as we pulled into Palm Springs, but I was able to fall back to sleep once the train got moving again. I didn't dare take the cover off my eyes now, lest my neighbor feel the need to speak to me again. I had no desire to face her incessant talking this morning. I was used to quiet so early in the morning, so I kept my mask on until we pulled into the station.

I was relieved to find that she'd already gone when I stood up to fold Grandma's quilt and tuck it under my arm so I could carry my handbag in one hand and my train case in the other. I collected my luggage and saw to it that a porter would have it on the train to Portland that would be arriving in a few hours.

I had about five hours to wait until departure. My first mission was to locate a toilet to ease the pressure on my bladder, which was quite considerable since I had not left my seat on the train for about nine hours. Next, I went in search of strong black coffee, which was not difficult, since there was a small countertop diner right in the station.

Feeling more awake, I found a coin operated locker to keep my things in and went for a long walk around the neighborhood. My joints were so stiff from sitting in one position through the night, that I needed to stretch my legs and move. I just walked with no destination in mind but to arrive back at Union Station in time to catch my train to Portland.

The air outside the station was fresh and moist. I reveled in the crisp air that one just didn't feel in Phoenix much after March or April, when the air was always warm and usually dry, until the monsoons brought humidity to the valley. There wasn't much call then for a sweater when going out anywhere.

I came across Los Angeles's City Hall and strolled through a large park before coming to a Catholic cathedral. Being Protestant, I was aware that I didn't know how to do the ritual motions properly, and I wondered whether I should go in. I decided that God would forgive me for not doing it correctly, and I stepped inside the dark, warm, cavernous church. I moved around the sanctuary until I spotted a side chapel. It was small and intimate. I lit a candle for my father, and I prayed for strength and peace for my mother. And for myself. I sat in the silence for a while, blotting my face of the tears that resumed once I allowed myself to remember why I was on this journey.

When I finally went back outside, the sun had risen in the sky and so had the temperature. I took off my sweater and carried it as I approached a block of old adobe houses that had seen better days but were still charming and illuminated by brilliant bougainvillea blossoms in spite of the peeling paint. I came to a fountain and stood in the generous shade of a tree and watched the water play, mesmerized by the hypnotic burbling coming from its flow. I didn't want to sit on any of the benches nearby, since I had nearly 30 hours of sitting ahead of me on the next leg of my journey. I kept walking, and I made it back to the station in time to use the facilities, collect my belongings out of the locker, and board the train.

Settling into my seat as the train pulled out of the station, I flipped through my LIFE magazine. Nothing in particular caught my eye, so I opened my LOOK magazine instead. I hadn't yet focused my eyes on the page when my mind wandered back to thoughts of my parents and to memories of my younger self. What if I had chosen differently? How different would my life be if I had just patiently waited for Johnny and not felt the need to be entertained and taken out by other boys?

I may have been pinned, but Johnny was away at college. He stipulated that we were steady when he was home from college, so we both understood that we could date other people when he was not home. He wrote me letters, and when he came home for the holidays, I only went out with him. While he was in Corvallis studying Engineering at Oregon state, and doing his duty in the National Guard, other boys invited me out. I figured there would be no harm done as long as I didn't kiss them.

I made sure the fellows knew about Johnny, and when they realized I wasn't really free to give my heart to them, a few stopped calling for dates, like George Iwata, who was in our high school class.

I heard that not long after the Japanese attack on our navy in Pearl Harbor, government agents searched George's parents' home, confiscating things like maps and cameras. Some people in the community expressed fear that the Japanese-American community was plotting with the Japanese government to attack the American homeland and destroy infrastructure like Bonneville Dam.

I couldn't imagine it was true; George and his brothers were as American as I and my siblings. He and his older brothers were born in Washington, and none of them had ever been to Japan. He had to leave with his family when President Roosevelt signed Executive Order 9066, forcing all Japanese-Americans to relocate on just 10 days' notice. We didn't know where his family went. I lost track of George after that.

One of the boys did keep calling, however. Dick Ellstrom was the most regular visitor who came around while Johnny was away. Actually, he came around when Johnny was home as well. In fact, he followed us and spied on us when we were on our dates, as he had done at the movies. Dick showed up at the sweet shoppe where we were having Cokes, and he just happened to ride his bicycle by us slowly as we were picnicking on Mt. Tabor. There was that open-air concert by the river that he happened to be at, alone. Too many coincidences for them to really be coincidences. In later years, his younger sister, Janet, told me that he was indeed following us despite her admonishments to leave us alone.

I went out with Dick when Johnny was not home because he asked, and I had nothing better to do. It was all quite innocent. Dick was nice enough, but sometimes he acted a little young compared to Johnny even though we were all the same age. His reactions to things seemed overly dramatic at times. He seemed to think that there was more between us than just friendship, but he never brought it up with me. He never asked me to be his steady and he never tried to put a pin on me. But then, he didn't belong to a fraternity, either.

Mom and Dad never commented about him. They were polite to him when he came to call on me, but they never offered him a seat or invited him to stay for a meal like they did with Johnny.

The night my father left for his mother's funeral, Mom asked if I wanted to go with her to my sister's to take care of baby Linda while Luella and Roy were at BINGO. I just wanted to stay home and go to bed early. I was in no mood to play with the baby, and I had to be at work in the morning anyway. She blew me a kiss when Roy honked for her, and she pulled the front door shut behind her.

It was just a moment after I heard the car drive off that there was a knock on the door. It was Dick.

"Do you want to go to the movies, Beth?"

"Aw, thanks, Dick, but I'm tired and I'm feeling sad about my Grandma. I just want to stay home tonight."

"All right. I'll just come in for a minute and sit with you."

Before I could say no and shut the door, he pushed past me and sat on my parents' living room couch. I didn't want to argue and force him to go, so I turned on the radio so we could hear some big band music. I sat on the couch with him.

We listened for a little bit, and I couldn't help but think how if it were Johnny here with me, he would have me up dancing. Weariness washed over me, so I turned to Dick to say, "I'm so tired, Dick. I—"

"Beth, I'm sorry about your grandmother. When is the funeral?"

"Oh, she lived in Nebraska, so my father is on his way there right now. He went by train, and he should get there in time for the funeral."

"Where's your mother tonight?"

"She's at my sister's wa—"

"Beth, I really like you, you know," he had interrupted me to say this. I just couldn't tolerate this. Not tonight. His timing was horrible.

"I do know, Dick, and I like you, too."

"No, I mean I really like you. I enjoy spending time with you."

"I do, too. I appreciate you taking me out when Johnny is away." I included Johnny in our conversation to remind Dick that I was not exactly available.

"About that, Beth. I don't like Johnny."

"Well, I do, Dick. He is a good man. He treats me well."

"But he's not here, is he?"

"No. Right now he's at National Guard combat training."

I was starting to get uncomfortable, and I moved to stand up. Dick grabbed my hand and forced me to stay sitting next to him. He looked at me with an intensity that I had to look away from.

"I want to kiss you, Beth."

"I don't think that would be a good idea, Dick."

He wrapped his arm around my waist and pulled me closer to him on the couch. Then he put his lips on mine. At first, I tried to pull away from him, but he held my head to his.

He stopped for a moment, then leaned his forehead on mine.

"Just a kiss, Beth."

His voice was soft, and his blue eyes looked into mine. He was smiling at me. I relaxed a little and he kissed me again. His lips were gentle and warm on mine, and it was comforting to be held. He smelled good. He had just shaved. I relaxed a bit more and found myself kissing him back. My stomach had butterflies tickling me from the inside, and I let him continue.

His hands were gently pulling me closer to him, when I remembered that this was not Johnny, who's steady I was. I didn't want Dick to get the wrong idea. My parents were not at home, and we shouldn't have been doing what we were doing.

My body stiffened again, and when I pulled away from him, Dick's face got red, and suddenly he exploded in anger.

"Do not pull away from me!"

Dick grabbed me and shifted my body so that I was on my back on the couch and he was on top of me. He was not touching me gently now. All tenderness was gone as he pinned me in a much different way than Johnny did when we flirted and roughhoused.

"What are you doing?"

He forced my silence with a determined kiss. He held my hands down as I struggled against him, and I realized he was much stronger than I was. I couldn't move, and I couldn't move him off me.

"Please, Dick. Don't," I said, but he didn't hear me. I tried to look in his eyes, to make him see me, but he was not there. The Dick I knew was gone, and this aggressive stranger was forcing himself on me in a way I'd never experienced before.

"Don't!" I yelled, but it was too late. He had overpowered me, pulled my skirt up, moved my panties aside, and now he was taking my body.

When he was done, he laid his head on the cushion next to mine, and he just breathed for a minute. I felt suffocated. I tried to move, and suddenly, Dick was back with me, politely asking whether he was crushing me. He pulled out of me and off of me without apology and sat next to me, smiling as he pulled his zipper up. I straightened my skirt over my knees as I sat up.

Why was he smiling? For some reason, I tried to smile back, but my face felt wooden. I tried to understand what was going on. What had just happened? I tried to find the answer in his face.

Dick was just looking at me, taking in my face. What information was he getting from my expression? I froze when he leaned over and kissed me. I didn't know what to say. I didn't know what to do. He was gentle again, but I feared him. I could feel my heart beating fast in my chest; the rush of blood was loud in my ears.

"That was nice, Beth. Thank you for allowing me to spend this evening with you. I know you are sad about your grandmother."

I didn't understand him. He had just taken me, roughly, and he was behaving like nothing had happened. He was acting like I had been a willing party to it. I couldn't utter a word. I stood up, and he stood with me. We walked to the door, and he said good-night.

I shut the door behind him, feeling sore, feeling numb. I tasted blood where his mouth had crushed my lip on my tooth.

I started to question myself. How had I led him on? Had I asked for that? I had enjoyed kissing him, until I remembered we were alone.

I asked him to stop. Maybe he didn't hear me. Maybe I didn't say it loud enough. Maybe I didn't even say it out loud. Maybe...

It was my fault. What else was he supposed to think? I let him into the house and then allowed him to stay with me when I was alone. I had sat next to him on the couch when I should have taken the chair. I should have worn a longer skirt. I should have buttoned the top button on my blouse. It was all my fault.

I turned out all but one light in the living room and went into the bathroom. My heart was racing, and my hands were shaking. I looked at myself in the mirror. It was still the same face I looked at every day, but I was different now. Dick had left no visible mark on me, but he had changed me somehow. I felt insecure for the first time in my life.

I drew a warm bath and tried to wash him off of me, scrubbing and scrubbing with the soapy washcloth. When I went to bed, I couldn't fall asleep. I couldn't turn off the thoughts in my head. Mother came home and must have seen that my lights were out. I was grateful she decided not to disturb me as she went right to bed.

Was the front door locked? I went out to double check, tiptoeing quietly, avoiding the squeaky floorboards so my mother wouldn't get up and want to talk to me. I couldn't face her right now. I just wanted to make sure we were safely locked in.

We never locked our door, but I thought it should be secured in case he came back in the night. And then I locked the back door. I had never been afraid before, but even though I heard my mother's sleeping breath in the next room and I knew I wasn't alone in the house, I was afraid that night.

I felt bad. I was a bad girl. I shouldn't have led Dick on like I had. Why, oh why had I kissed him? Why, oh why had I enjoyed kissing him? What would I tell Johnny?

Johnny didn't need to ever know. I would talk to Dick and…

And what? Ask him not to say anything to anyone? I doubted he'd do that anyway. Maybe I would never see him again.

Then I started to get angry. Dick knew I was with Johnny. He'd followed us around enough to know that Johnny and I were serious about each other. But then I kissed Dick. If I was truly serious about Johnny, why would I have kissed Dick? And then I pulled away from him, and he got so angry with me when I did. I must have really hurt his feelings.

Eventually, I fell into a fitful sleep, but when I awoke in the morning, my heart was heavy. I wanted to cry. I left earlier than usual for work, with my head full of conflicting thoughts and self-doubt.

I punched my timecard as I left work that evening, not wanting to face my mother, yet I had no other plan but to go home to her. It would be fine. I would just ask her about baby Linda, and then she would be so caught up in stories about her, that she wouldn't ask about me. That sounded just fine.

As I walked out the exit door, I saw that Dick was waiting for me with the other men, husbands and beaux of my co-workers, fellow operators at the phone company. My stomach immediately flipped around inside of me, and my heart started pounding, but I kept walking toward him with the other girls.

Dick had a big smile on his face, and he held out a bouquet of flowers to me. They must have cost a pretty penny, since it was not yet springtime. It was well before flowers really started blooming unless they were raised in a hothouse, or a warmer climate before being shipped up to Portland.

In spite of myself, I smiled. He told me, "I missed you today," and he kissed me tenderly on my mouth.

I didn't want to slap him in public and make a scene, so I held off. A couple of the girls I worked with walked past with puzzled looks on their faces. I could tell they were wondering who this fellow was and what happened to Johnny, but they didn't stop to ask me. I kind of wished they would. I didn't know what Dick had planned, and I had a dry mouth and a belly full of butterflies.

We started walking in silence. After a block, he said, "I'm sorry about last night, Beth. I realized after I left that I wasn't the nicest guy, and I want to make it up to you."

"What happened, Dick? Did I make you cross? I didn't mean to hurt your feelings."

"No, you didn't, Beth. It's OK."

What did he think was OK? Nothing was OK. I felt confused, but I didn't know how to talk with him.

"Are you hungry, Beth? Can I take you to dinner?"

I was hungry, and even though I just wanted to go home, I felt like maybe more time with him would help clear things up for me. I didn't understand what had happened. And the flowers were so beautiful, and he was being such a gentleman. I must have been wrong last night when I felt scared of him.

"Sure, Dick. I could eat a little something."

We stepped into a diner and took a table by the window. We ordered our food: meatloaf for me, and beef stew for him. We talked about nothing, and he talked about everything. He told me about his job at the power company, which he said was fine, but what Dick really wanted to do was go to college at the University of Oregon in Corvallis and become an engineer. *Like Johnny*, I thought. He wanted to have a family and travel some. He asked if I wanted those things, too.

"I do, Dick. Johnny and I have talked a lot about that."

He stiffened and looked at me. I could see the rage coming up in his eyes again.

"I wasn't talking about Johnny."

"I know, Dick. I know."

"You're with ME now, Beth. There's no going back to Johnny. You have to let him know you are with me now."

I looked at him. I was shocked. He was right, of course. I'd been to the place with Dick that Johnny and I had wanted to go many times, but we held back, understanding that once we were married, we could go all the way together. I realized now that Johnny and I would never do that, of course.

Dick was right. He had claimed me last night. He had made my decision for me. Now my future had to be with him, not with Johnny.

"Of course, Dick. I know."

I noticed that people were starting to watch us. I didn't want any attention, so I smiled at him and touched his hand, hoping to calm him. Somehow it worked. He smiled back at me and relaxed. He continued to eat, but I felt sick to my stomach. I couldn't eat anymore, so I watched him, and although I could barely hear him for the thoughts racing around in my mind, I nodded as he talked more about what he wanted in life. How he wanted our life to be together.

I felt like my fate was sealed. I felt like I had somehow lost sight of the shore, and I was being carried out to sea, unable to steer or row, adrift in the current and riding the swelling waves alone, descending into that low, low trough, mountainous waves above me on both sides, ready to collapse over me.

The pit of my stomach had that nauseating sensation like when I swing so high on a swing that it loses tension at the peak dropping point and falls back into its return arc, or when I sled too fast down a steep, snowy hill and dip at the bottom before coming to a stop at the next hill.

I gripped the sides of my chair to try to control my nerves, but it didn't work. I looked around, and even though the diner was full of people, there was no one there. No one to throw me a lifeline. No one to help me.

Oh, why hadn't I gone to Luella and Roy's with Mother last night? I should have been with her anyway because she was feeling sad about Grandma Lydia.

I was second-guessing myself and trying to figure out how to get out of this with Dick, even while he was talking away. He didn't ask me questions; he simply looked to me for affirmation, and when I nodded, that apparently was good enough for him.

Finally, he finished eating and noticed I hadn't finished my meal. "What's wrong, Beth? You barely touched your dinner. I'm paying good money for that. We'd better get a doggy bag. You can take it for lunch tomorrow."

I nodded once more and excused myself to go to the restroom. I hung my head over the toilet and flushed down what little I had eaten.

On the way home, I began to cry, and when Dick put his arm around me and comforted me, he must have assumed I was sad about my Grandma Lydia.

"Santa Barbara, next station, Santa Barbara."

People around me were gathering their belongings to get off the train, and there were many unoccupied seats, so I decided to find one on the other side of the train so I could better see the coast and the Pacific Ocean as we continued north.

Pulling out of the station, the man who had taken a seat across from me pulled out a sandwich and started eating. My stomach started to growl, and the hunger pangs reminded me that here it was midday of Saturday, and I hadn't eaten since dinner with Dick and the kids Thursday night.

Once we were underway, I collected my things and made my way to the diner car, where I sat at a table covered with a white linen cloth. The tuna melt on wheat I ordered came quickly, but I took my time eating it as I looked out the window at the ocean vista. Once the tracks took us inland, my mind wandered back to 1942.

Dad was gone for one week, but it felt like a month. I was so happy when he came home, and Mother wanted to know every detail about Grandma Lydia's funeral and about all of their friends and family there.

I used spending time with my father as an excuse to not see Dick every day, as had become our routine. He would pick me up every night from work and take me to dinner, and then he took me home and dropped me off at the door. He didn't try to come into the house again. He didn't try to do anything more than hold my hand and kiss me when we were together.

In my head, I reconciled being with him in spite of what he'd done to me because I couldn't exactly do anything about it now. Who could I tell, anyway? I was so ashamed and felt that the blame was all mine. No one would understand, and they would only confirm that I was to blame. People had seen us together, and I was always willing to be with him before. They would think I had no grounds for complaint against him. They would think I had loose morals, and that I might just sleep with boys even though we weren't married, or at the very least lead them on. I was not that kind of girl. My parents did not raise me to be that way. I couldn't let them down.

Because Dick didn't try anything more with me, I thought I could just go along with him until he grew bored with me and moved on to another girl. As the weeks wore on, however, that didn't happen. He just seemed to be more enamored with me, the more time we spent together.

Dick did make being with him easy. Being admired and appreciated and cared for was endearing, and after a while, I couldn't be angry with him anymore. In moments of quiet and solitude, I still resented what he did to me, and I kept my guard up around him, just in case I had to fight him off, but over time, his compliments and flowers softened my hard feelings.

On the weekends, Dick took me for picnics on Mount Tabor. He found an intimate grove sheltered all around by ancient tall trees. It kept others from seeing us. He said that we were safe from others' prying eyes, but I felt vulnerable in being invisible to others. I breathed a sigh of relief each time we emerged from the little circle back into the open park.

"One day we'll live on this mountain, Beth. In Montebello. Would you like that?"

Despite my underlying sense of unease, I nodded. For the first time, I felt like I would actually like that. Montebello was a charming, village-like neighborhood. It was so beautiful on Mount Tabor and so quiet.

When Mother realized that I was seeing Dick as a steady, she asked how Johnny had taken the news. I realized that it was time to write Johnny a letter. I had to do it. It was the saddest letter I ever wrote. I returned his pin, sending it with the tear-stained letter. I never heard from Johnny again. I understand he survived the war and married a redhead named Bertha.

A few months after my Grandma Lydia died, my clothes were not fitting me quite right, and then I realized that two months had passed since my last cycle, since that night that Dick overpowered me in my parents' living room. It had only been one time. I couldn't possibly have gotten pregnant from that one time.

I became scared, and after a few days of going over it again and again in my mind, hoping for things to return to normal, I realized I'd have to tell someone. I'd have to go to the doctor to find out for sure. If I actually was pregnant, I'd have to tell everyone.

The doctor confirmed what I feared. When I told Dick, he seemed overjoyed, once his initial shock and disbelief wore off. But then he got angry and started asking me about Johnny. Had I written to him to let him know I was with Dick now? When was the last time I saw him? Had we slept together?

Somehow I convinced Dick that I hadn't seen Johnny since he was home for Christmas, and no, Johnny and I had never been intimate in that way. Because he had been with me every moment I wasn't at work or with my parents, Dick finally believed that the baby was his. I reminded him that we had to marry immediately.

"It's been a couple of months already, Dick, so the sooner the better."

"Of course, of course, Beth. Let's go talk to your pastor today."

We went to Grace Baptist Church, where I attended with my family, and we scheduled a modest ceremony to take place the very next day, May 14, with only my sister and my best friend, Jean, as witnesses.

Pastor Milliken asked no questions of us, and I think he assumed our rush was in light of the war and the fact that many young men were enlisting in the military and going off for training.

That evening, when I told my mother I was going to marry Dick, she asked no questions. I think she knew.

When our little baby was born six months later, everyone would know. There was nothing to talk about, and I was certainly doing the right thing by marrying the father of my baby. Any other course of action would have brought shame upon me and my family. I had an obligation to give my baby a name, his father's name.

I shut the door to my room after dinner as I packed a bag to go with Dick the next day. I wept as I came to the realization that I had no choice but to love this man, and I resolved to devote my life to him and be a good wife. I wanted to be happy, and I believed that decision would eventually bring me happiness.

Dick told me that when he told his parents, his father insisted on him saving $1000 and having it in the bank before getting married, but we could not wait.

We got married, according to plan, on a Thursday afternoon. The ceremony was very brief, and after we all signed the certificate, Dick and I got in his car and immediately headed off on our honeymoon with no celebration or fanfare.

We spent the next few days slowly driving up and down both sides of the Columbia Gorge, stopping at waterfalls and walking on trails. At night, we stayed in whichever little inn we came across after dinner.

Besides that one time, Dick was kind to me before we were married, making sure all my needs were met. Now that we were married, and especially after he learned of my delicate condition, he was very careful with me, and let me barely lift a finger when it came to carrying luggage or opening doors. He was tender with me in the bedroom, too.

Our favorite place we found was a little town called Apple Grove. The wide river was visible all along the road, and from everywhere in the township, we could hear it flowing toward the Pacific Ocean.

We were so happy when Dick's work moved us to Apple Grove just as soon as our first week together as man and wife was over. It was a sweet place to start our life. True to its name, there were apple trees everywhere, and as it turned out, apples were all I was hungry for as my belly grew bigger and bigger. I ate so many tart green apples, that Dick would tease me, "We're not going to have a baby, you're cooking me an apple pie in there!"

Once I'd made my decision to give my future to Dick, my outlook changed, and I was able to relax more with him, especially as he proved that his one violent claiming act was an anomaly. I grew to love Dick more and more deeply all the time. He loved me with enough passion that he made up for whatever lack of love for him I may have had at first. He was kind to me as long as I didn't make him angry.

Although he could be quiet and moody, Dick made me laugh, and he shared his thoughts and dreams with me. Dick respected my father, and Dick's actions showed me that he desired Dad's approval very much, even sharing his ideas with him and asking for his advice.

Unfortunately, he was not as forthcoming with anyone else. It took him a while to warm up to people, so he didn't have the numbers of friends and the close relationships with them that I did. He was uncomfortable around people until he had spent a lot of time with them. I think my friends wondered why I had chosen Dick when John—who was more social, like me—seemed a better match and a better fit within our circle.

I decided that since my life was going to be with Dick, I would enjoy the side of him that he only shared with me. Being loved so deeply by Dick endeared him to me, but even more endearing were the vulnerabilities that I soon learned drove his idiosyncratic social behavior and his occasional rages. I began to see that the fear and jealousy he acted on came from a hurt heart, and I wanted to protect his heart and give him the love he so craved and reassure him that the love, my love, that he so feared he would lose was not going anywhere. My feelings for Dick deepened each day, so it was with sincere fear in my heart that I realized I could possibly lose him to war.

Dick had boasted he was one of the first in line to sign up for the draft after Japan bombed Pearl Harbor, so it wasn't a complete surprise when he got his induction letter the first week of October 1942. He read the message aloud to me.

"'*From the president of the United States. Greeting.*' Look, Beth. They left off the 's.'"

Grammatical and spelling errors annoyed Dick, "Especially in correspondence from the president," he told me, "'*Having submitted yourself to a local board, you are hereby notified that you have been selected.*'"

He had a week and a half before he had to report to the draft board, and from what our friends and brothers who had already enlisted told us, we knew that if he was accepted when he reported, he would have just under three weeks to get his affairs in order before he left for basic training with the Navy. Dick went to his boss at the Western Electric Company and showed him the letter, so he would have a job waiting when he returned, whether that be the next day or in a few years.

Dick was not a student, he was five-feet-eight inches tall, and his vision was 20/20. He could think of no reason they would not accept him into service, so we prepared for a long deployment.

"I want to go back to work while you are away, Dick."

"I won't hear of it, Beth. The military will send compensation for you and for the baby once he arrives, so you don't have to worry about money, especially if you will be staying at our parents' homes."

To save money and to have help with the baby, we gave up the Apple Grove house, and moved in with his parents. I arranged to stay with Mother and Daddy once Dick left for basic training in San Francisco. It eased my mind knowing that when my labor began, they could get me to a hospital in time.

I was happy to be with my parents again. I had my old bedroom, which Mother hadn't changed much in the few months I'd been gone.

Daddy snored so loudly that he still slept in another bedroom down the hall. It was better for his back anyway because the mattress he slept on was much firmer than Mother's.

One night after we had all gone to bed, I was just drifting off to sleep when I heard Daddy's door creak open. His socks muffled the sound of his feet padding down the hallway until they reached Mother's door. His knuckle rapped twice and then the glass doorknob squeaked as he turned it. I heard the door shut, and the knob squeaked again.

I turned over to my side, tucking a pillow between my legs to ease the pressure on my hips, when I heard Mother's giggles and Daddy's low teasing voice. Then a slow rhythmic metallic friction that was punctuated by another giggle, and then silence until a banging against the wall made me sit up, startled. I realized her iron headboard was striking the wall behind it like a drum with a steadily increasing tempo until sighs and groans gave way to silence. I started to giggle and brought a pillow up to my face so they wouldn't hear me. And then Mother's giggle joined Daddy's low voice.

They must have forgotten I was home, for I had never heard them making love before. Perhaps they thought the walls were thicker. Maybe they didn't care that I heard now that I was a married lady myself.

It felt better to sit up, so I walked to the dresser in the bluish light of the moon shining through the window over the curtain. I poured myself a glass of water from the pitcher Mother left for me on the dresser.

A framed picture of Dick and myself smiled up at me. I tried to imagine him sleeping under a scratchy, government-issue wool blanket on a narrow cot in a room full of other fellows, some of whom also had wives sleeping somewhere else alone. I missed my husband.

I looked at myself in the mirror. My auburn hair was pinned up in an effort to control which way the curls would go in the morning. I turned to the side to see how big my belly was becoming. I ran my left hand over the bump and rocked it back and forth, shifting on my bare feet.

Mother's doorknob creaked again, and the door bounced against the frame as Daddy pulled it to. He padded down the hall into his own bedroom. Mother's faint but audible wheezes told me she had fallen into a satisfied sleep.

Although I was feeling lonely, I had a smile on my face as I got back into my bed and shut my eyes.

Our little girl was born when Dick was away at basic training in California. We had talked about names, and Nancy Delores was the one we had decided on for a daughter. We expected a boy to come first, but I was so happy that I didn't care that we were wrong.

When Dick wrote back to tell me he'd gotten the happy news in my Dad's telegram, I was relieved that he seemed happy about having a girl.

He reminded me that his parents were eager to help with the baby, and I appreciated that because my mother was not as young as she once was, so I didn't want her bearing the full burden of caring for us on top of helping Luella with her little girl, who was quite busy and demanding of attention.

Dick and I had been looking forward to our first Christmas together, but that would not happen now as he was immersed in his first leg of training to become a Naval Radio Technician. None of the men in his division were granted leave to be with their families even though they were still stateside.

Having just had our baby, I couldn't travel to see him, but Daddy took pictures of me with the baby to send to Dick, and we planned for me to go stay with him on base in the spring. He got family housing there, and I left Nancy with our parents. Dick was so happy to finally meet our little girl when he came home for a week that summer.

It wasn't long after he came home that my husband was moved to Maryland, where the ship he was assigned to was christened, and he wrote that they had actually gone out to sea in test runs while he was in training.

Luckily, it was possible for me to go where he was stationed stateside when he had leaves during his long training period. Of course, he wanted me to be available to travel to him and then stay a few days, and I was only too glad to go, for I didn't want those khaki-wacky girls paying any attention to my husband.

"Stay away from those Victory girls, Dick. You just wait for me to get there."

"Beth, darling, you have to be ready at a moment's notice. The military makes decisions and then delivers the message. There may be a time frame, but the command may not come down at any given specific time."

So I kept a bag packed, and so did he. I left Nancy with Mother and Dad, and they shared the care of her with Dick's parents. I traveled whenever I could to be with Dick for as long as I could stay. I felt lucky to have him stateside, where I knew he was safe, but I realized that once his ship was christened, and trainings were done, he would be going to sea to fight either the Japanese or the Germans.

His brothers-in-law were already deployed. His older sister Evelyn's husband, Howard, was in the South China Sea. His service involved operating his ship's radar system. Janet was their baby sister, and her husband John was in Europe serving as an Army Air Force bombardier, stationed in England and flying missions over Germany.

Dick was able to come home one last time before going to his final training assignment before he was deployed. After five months in North Carolina, and nearly two years after his enlistment, he finally set sail out of Virginia on the communications ship, McKinley. He shipped out to the Pacific, and I knew I wouldn't be seeing my husband back at home for a long time.

If I took Dick's letters to me at their word, it would seem that my husband was on an extended pleasure cruise around the Pacific Ocean. The letters I collected and tied up in a silky green ribbon were very sparse, with no details of actual warfare. I liked that just fine.

Nevertheless, it was a war zone, and the thought of Dick in the middle of the ocean scared me. I feared I'd lose him.

I enjoyed his descriptions of the day-to-day on the ship, both mundane and noteworthy. He told me what happened when his ship crossed the Equator a few days out from Hawaii.

"We all knew there would be an initiation, and a mock court was set up with Neptune and Davy Jones. Suddenly, this mob of fellows jumped on us, Beth, calling us 'pollywogs' and beating us black and blue. Next, they gave us razors and forced us to shave our legs. They dumped big barrels of paint on us, and then we had to line up to receive a shock with a generator wire. That wasn't all, Beth, but in the end, I got my official certificate signed by Neptune and Davy Jones. Your husband is now officially a Shellback."

He described the loneliness of the seemingly endless ocean, and the beauty of the tropical islands they came across, and the star-filled skies at night.

The irony of Dick being in the Navy was that he didn't know how to swim. He let me know that he had learned by necessity.

"The fellows and I were on shore leave in the Philippine Islands. It's beautiful there, Beth. One night, we'd had a bit to drink, and we all started swimming the short distances from one island to another. With the full moon our only source of light, it was either go along or be left behind. So I went along."

We heard on the radio about drawn-out battles being fought on islands in the South Pacific. We saw on the newsreels the tenacity of our Japanese foes as the Allies closed in on Japan, taking control of island after island in the Island-Hopping Campaign, forcing the Japanese to retreat to defend their homeland. I was so grateful that Dick's job as a Radio Technician kept him on the ship, not having to face the enemy in person.

By the time our men reached Japan, I knew they'd be heavily targeted.

Once Dick was home, he told me that his ship was part of a large force of ships that traveled together. They were under constant threat of air attacks and at any moment, they knew they could be sunk by a kamikaze plane from the sky, or by a torpedo from the depths below. He saw ships on either side of the McKinley get blown to bits and sink, leaving the men from those ships to try and survive in shark-infested water that was aflame from all the leaked petroleum.

"You'd think that water should put out the fire, Beth, but it didn't. There was too much oil in the water, so the men who were not taken down by the sharks burned to death, and we had to listen to their screams. There was nothing we could do for them."

Although he didn't look at me, I took his hand. I didn't say anything, and he continued, "For some reason, my ship was never hit, Beth. I just can't figure out how we were never hit. I don't think we were praying any harder than any of the guys on those ships that didn't make it. We were just incredibly lucky."

Dick's ship came back to San Francisco in June 1945, and I spent the last summer of the war with him on Mare Island, the naval base northeast of the San Francisco Bay. It was an uncertain time, for we didn't know if and when Dick's ship would be called back to active service in the Pacific. The end of the war was near, we just didn't know when we would finally have peace again.

Early one warm August morning, I heard the Chronicle drop on our doorstep. I went to bring it in so I could fish the crossword puzzle out of it before Dick took the paper into the bathroom with him.

"Japan Hit by Atom Bomb — Mightiest Weapon in History!
Tokyo Admits Heavy Damage"

I couldn't believe it took a single atomic bomb to wipe out an entire city. And America had to do this twice before the Japanese surrendered. Dick could believe it.

"They don't believe in surrender, Beth. They'd rather die than lose."

The next week, when the peace was announced, I wrote to Mother and Daddy about how we celebrated VJ Day.

"First, we heard a girl scream and then we heard the whistles. A girl from across the way came over and told us the war was over. We went outside, and everyone was out there yelling. Everyone was well-stocked with liquor, so at two and three a.m. we could still hear them. Our neighbors, another young couple, came for dinner with their baby, and we celebrated with Cokes. We really had a very nice time. Just as we got in bed, we heard someone at the front door, and it was a telegram from Dick's mother. It is wonderful, and I only hope that Dick won't have to go out to sea again."

My hopes were dashed the week after that, when Dick's ship was called to participate in the occupation of Japan. He sailed west, and I headed north, back to Portland to continue waiting for my husband to come home.

Thankfully, Dick's stay in Yokohama was only a few months, so he sailed back to the States and was discharged from the Navy. He made it home just in time for our first Christmas together as a family.

Dick had only been able to spend short amounts of time with our daughter when he came home on leave three times during his training. Nancy had just turned three when he arrived home for the last time. She didn't remember him at first. Dick was so disappointed that she cried when we took her from her grandmother's home, that I think he felt some resentment toward her. I found him scowling at her one day, and I used a light-hearted tone as I reminded him that she was just a baby and would grow to know and love him. He agreed with me, but

I still felt Dick's jealousy when I would take care of Nancy. I gave him enough attention that he seemed to get over it in time.

When our boy Jim was born, Dick was so happy to have a son. He still expected me to devote most of my attention to him, though. Luckily, Nancy was big enough that she could feed her baby brother with a bottle, and she gave him his meals when he was old enough to eat solid food, so I could spend more time with Dick.

We soon became immersed in our family life, spending time with relatives; going to the beach; going up to Mt. Hood to play in the snow or to spend time at the family cabin; bridge parties with friends; dinner parties with friends; Nancy's Girl Scout activities.

The war became a distant memory for us, well for me anyway. Dick didn't tell me if he still thought about it, but I figured he did from time to time when he got short-tempered and shouted at me.

The Harts were our best friends. Fred and Norma moved their family when we moved ours, first to Chicago and then to Baltimore. Fred and Dick worked together and got transferred together. They were a touchstone for us as we left Portland, the only home we had ever known. I think we were that for them as well.

Their four boys—Ricky, Billy, Larry, and Stanley—were close with Nancy and Jim. I was proud of how Nancy held her own with that pack. They were wild, and they all played hard.

Norma was a tiny woman, but she wrangled her brood better than I could have. When things got very heated and the boys started doing real damage in the house, she would order them all to the basement and tell them to put on their gloves and go to the mats. That seemed to bring peace to her household, temporary as it may be.

Norma and I spent time in the afternoons after our housekeeping and errands were done. We had everything in common, so our conversations were easy and ongoing, even as we played endless card games, drinking light spritzers and smoking all afternoon until the kids and our husbands came home.

We vacationed together, renting a big house on a lake. With five bedrooms, there was plenty of space for all of us to be comfortable for a week. Nancy was the only girl, so she got her own room, and Jim and Larry shared a room. They were the same age and inseparable. The other three Hart boys shared the other bedroom with a bunk bed and a twin bed in it.

There was a generous covered porch where we could gather while the kids went swimming. As long as they were making noise, we knew they were OK.

One day, I realized I was not hearing Nancy. Norma and I looked toward the lake at the same time to see the five boys taking turns dunking Nancy. She seemed to be struggling. Norma yelled, "Fred!"

He looked where she was pointing and took in the situation. He stood up just as we saw Billy stop the other boys and help Nancy back to the shore. I stepped off the porch to go make sure my daughter was all right and Norma went with me.

Nancy was coughing and having a hard time catching her breath. Norma grabbed her arms and held them above her head. She stopped coughing and laid back on the rocky shore.

"I'm OK," she said, smiling. "Thanks, Billy. I think you saved my life."

"Don't mention it," he said, and ran back into the water with his brothers and Jim.

We shared so many good times that we became like family. Even Dick was relatively happy when he was with them, so we drove the 45-minute distance between us in Maryland to see them often. It was so hard to leave them when we moved to Phoenix. They didn't want to go to yet another place, so they returned home to Oregon, settling in Salem. I really wished that we were returning there as well, but going to the southwest was good for Dick's career so that was the move we made.

They did come to visit us. Once they came just after I had surgery on my back. I wouldn't have wanted a visit from anyone else at that time, but I knew that Norma could take care of her own family and I wouldn't have to do anything to host them. I needed to see them, and Nancy was old enough that she could step in for me and do the shopping and meals and cleaning.

The Harts had been at our house just a couple of days, when Dick came home and flew into a rage. He shoved me onto our bed and was yelling something about what a whore I was. He started hitting my face. I was in so much pain from my surgery that my efforts to fight him off were too weak. I screamed like I normally didn't do. I was afraid he was going to kill me. Fred came bursting through the bedroom door.

"Good God, Dick! What the hell are you doing?"

He pulled my husband off me and held him back from attacking me again. Norma came in and helped me to sit up, saying, "Shame on you, Dick. Beth just had surgery for God's sake."

He broke free from Fred and ran out the door. I could hear him sobbing in the backyard through our windows. I was so ashamed. I hadn't done anything to provoke him. I wasn't flirting with anyone, and Fred certainly wasn't flirting with me. I didn't have provocative clothes on.

"I'm so sorry, I don't know what came over him."

When I began to weep, Norma said, "Fred, go to the kitchen and get some ice for Beth's face."

Fred walked out looking stunned and red-faced.

"You have nothing to apologize for, Beth. You didn't do anything wrong, and you have nothing to be ashamed about. Dick is the brute, and that does not reflect on you."

"But it does. I tolerate it, and I let him hit the kids, too. I am so weak against him. I just don't know what to do, Norma. He is so unhappy."

"When is Dick ever happy? More importantly, Beth, when are you happy? You don't need to stay with him."

Oh, the thought was too horrible to consider. No one I knew was divorced. That would be too difficult. My sister had divorced her husband when their daughters were small. She'd gone to Michigan to be with Mother and Daddy, but when Roy followed them, she married him a second time and they had two little boys that the older girls helped take care of. Roy was loyal and worked hard to please Luella, and she could easily boss him around to do her bidding.

If I left Dick, I couldn't imagine going back to him. It would be over. Maybe I didn't want to fail at something I worked so hard for years to make succeed. I didn't want anyone to ever think I'd had to marry Dick. People liked and respected me, and that would change if I were a divorcee.

"I don't want to lose your friendship, Norma."

"You never will, Beth. We are here for you. Always."

Norma and Nancy got dinner together, and when Dick joined us at the table, he was contrite. "I'm sorry, Fred. I was out of line."

"I believe it's your wife who deserves that apology."

"You're right. I'm sorry, darling. Forgive me?"

I just nodded. I didn't believe a word he said. He'd be on me again after they left us. It may not be right away, but another attack would come.

"Approaching Davis. Davis, California."

I had gone back to the observation car after I finished my sandwich to have a couple of drinks and watch the rolling golden hills and vast green fields of California's Central Valley as we rolled by.

The world was darkening at dusk and would soon be too dark to observe much of anything at all. I put out my cigarette and returned to the passenger car to get a good seat and settle in for the long night ahead.

As the train pulled out of the station, I quickly drifted off to sleep. Before I knew it, the light of the rising sun flooded the rail car, and I opened my eyes to find night had given way to the day. My body was telling me to immediately go to pay the water bill. I made it to the restroom in perfect time because when I came out, there was already a line of ladies waiting to use it.

The sweet aroma of freshly brewed coffee awakened my senses, and I followed my nose to the diner car and bought my first cup of the day. I walked carefully back to my seat lest I spill a drop, and I enjoyed my black coffee with my morning cigarette.

Memories of my parents' spring visit came to mind. We were all on our best behavior for a week. I didn't have my first cocktail until 5 p.m. Mother didn't like drinking, but Dad joined me for one, and then I had a few more in my bedroom after they went to bed. Dick didn't go to the tennis club while they were here, which was a nice change, as he spent increasingly more and more time there instead of at home with us. He and Jim took my father golfing, and Nancy and I took Mother downtown to do some window shopping.

It was wonderful to be with them. I was happy to have them see more of where we live and spend time with us in our home. They had taken a winter road trip the year after we moved here, and we were finally moved into the house we had built on Calle del Paisano. They stayed with us for a week or so. Then they took a day trip to Tucson, visiting Mexico and Tombstone on the way back to Phoenix to spend a few more days before they drove back home to Portland.

This time, they flew, so there was less travel time for them, and they could spend more time with us. We got all caught up on the family news. For my parents, cousins were siblings and siblings were cousins. Being related to the same people, it made their extended family that much closer than other families we knew whose relatives were not as much a part of their lives as ours were.

We always took it for granted that anyone in the extended family had an open invitation to holidays or to any days, and most of the time we showed up when we could, for we were friends as well as relations. Not everyone was as fortunate as we were in that respect.

Rolling the ash of my cigarette into a conical tip on the metal ash-tray in the arm of my seat somehow reminded me of the conversation

I had with my dad the night before they left. The silvery moon had lit the night sky enough that I could watch the clouds move over our backyard as I sat on the back patio in my housecoat.

The sleeping house was dark and quiet when I slipped out to the back patio for a middle of the night smoke, so it startled me when the heavy glass door slowly slid open. My father's face peered out at me. We smiled at each other, and he stepped outside, pulling the door shut behind him. Curly, our dog, left patrolling of the fence line to run over to greet him. Standing next to me with his hands in his pockets, Dad said quietly, "I thought I got up early, but you've got me beat, Bess."

"I am up a bit earlier than usual."

When I said no more, he nodded and sat down next to me. He surprised me a second time when he reached for the pack of cigarettes and took one out. He placed it between his lips and held Dick's silver lighter to it, pulling the flame toward him as he sucked in air.

"Why, I don't recall ever seeing you smoke, Dad!"

He blew smoke out toward the shadowy yard and answered me, "Nope, I don't suppose you would. Mother doesn't like it, so I only have one every now and again."

It was my turn to nod as he sat back in his chair, taking another drag. He blew his smoke up to the stars. A cool breeze rustled the palm fronds above us, and we sat smoking in companionable silence. He put his hand down to stroke Curly's head, and I reached over to stub out my butt. I started to say, "We are loving having you and—", when he interrupted me.

"Yes, darling girl, we are very happy to visit you all here. Now tell me what's wrong."

Perhaps my dad thought it was too early in the morning for small talk, for he had cut through my pretense to get straight to the heart of the matter, and I had no answer for him.

"Whatever do you mean, Daddy?"

"Come on, Bess. Do you think I don't know my own daughter? I can feel the tension in this house. I can see you trying hard to make sure everything looks good, but you don't seem happy."

I knew he wouldn't let me fake my way out of it, so I took another cigarette out and stole a moment to light it. I blew out the sweet first smoke and began to apologize, "I'm sorry, Dad. I didn't want you or Mother to feel uncomfortable here. I wanted to give you no reason to worry about us."

"Worry. Should we be worried? What is there to worry about, Bess?"

"Nothing, Daddy. Nothing."

My father got quiet, seeming to ponder my denial.

"Dick's been trying hard, too. He has a temper, doesn't he?"

"Yes." I didn't want to get into the details with him, so I left it at that.

"Does he get violent, Bess, with you or the kids?"

"No, Daddy," I lied, looking down at the tiles on the mosaic table-top. In daylight, they were very bright and colorful, but they were only shades of gray in the darkness of night.

"He'd better not," he said simply.

"Dick admires and respects no one as much as you, Dad."

"Well…" my father seemed to have run out of words to say to that. He stubbed his cigarette out in the glass ashtray and looked me in the eyes.

"It's important, Bess, for you to make the most of it. You may feel like leaving, but remember that he's the man you chose to have a family with."

I looked away then. I hadn't chosen that. What I had chosen was to accept Dick's choice to join his life with mine, so that I could be happy, for I had no other choice. It had worked for a while.

"Your children need you to stay strong for them," my father went on. "They need you to make their home not only clean and comfortable, which you do a wonderful job of, but happy, too. Please remember that, Bess, when things are not rosy. I want you to be happy."

He spoke so earnestly, and to reassure him, I smiled, but my heart felt heavy. I had chosen to stay with Dick, and I chose to have another baby with him. It was not my choice to be yelled at and hit when his temper was set off.

Dad looked skyward and I did, too. The clouds were still floating past, obscuring and then opening our view of the stars. A gentle breeze rustled the trees and caressed my face as it blew past us.

"My mother left us once," he said quietly. "For some reason, she was deeply unhappy, and one day she was just gone. It was horrible, Bess. We worried and wondered for two years, until one day, she just came back."

I was so surprised, I had no words. I knew my grandmother wasn't a very happy person, but it never occurred to me to wonder why. It never crossed my mind to imagine her life outside of my limited experience of her. I thought back to the time when she visited us in Portland when I was a child. I took a tray up to her room for breakfast, for she liked to stay in bed long after our family had finished eating together in the kitchen. She pulled a nickel out of her red leather coin purse, and placing it in my little hand, she said, "A tip for good service." She smiled at me then, but her smile was not for me. She seemed very far away, and I felt alone when I was with her, so I didn't stay with her while she ate her eggs and toast. Did she live with a difficult man, like I did? Was she yelled at? Hit? Why did she go back?

My father continued his story, "she told us she'd been to see Aunt Dutch, but Aunt Dutch had been to see us, and said that she had no word from Mother. Father believed she'd taken up with the peddler that came around every year to sell us hardware and dry goods. After Mother left, that peddler never came back again, and we were never allowed to speak his name again. Father was devastated, Bess. He shrunk to half his size, is what he looked like."

I never wanted to disappoint my father. I would have to stay strong for him and tough it out with Dick. I found it interesting that he said his father shrunk to half his size because that was how I felt as Dick loomed over me with contempt in his eyes and vengeance in his fist, yet I never felt as small and powerless as when he raged at our children.

I would never share what really went on in our home. It was all my fault because I just couldn't make my husband happy, no matter what I did. When I bought his favorite brand of cigarettes, he said that I smoked too much. When he brought unexpected company home for dinner and I made a meal that knocked everyone's socks off, he said I flirted with his boss, or his client, or our friends' husbands too much. Although I made sure the backyard was free of dog poop, he complained that the dog barked too much, and then, in a fury, he'd kick the dog.

"Keep Curly out of Dad's way, Jim," I'd warn our son.

The laundry was always fresh, and I made sure all our clothes were neatly ironed so our family would always look our best, but he yelled when the kids left a magazine open on the couch instead of closed neatly on the coffee table.

"Were you raised in a barn?" he would rage at them. "I don't work hard all day to come home to a mess."

When I tried to make him happy in our bedroom and put on pretty lingerie I hoped he'd find seductive, he said that I was a whore, so he used me like I was one, and then he hit me and told me to sleep on the floor. I hid the bruises under my clothes or with makeup. I took aspirin to ease my physical pain. I masked my emotional pain with drinks.

He said that I drank too much, and on that count, he was probably right. I couldn't win with Dick, and I was nearing the end of my rope, but I would never tell my father. I would be such a disappointment to him.

Mother and Dad took oranges and grapefruit from our trees back to Oregon with them, and they had enough to share with their neighbors. The house felt empty when they went home. The kids were in school, and Dick spent more time at the club again. I played a lot of bridge, so I had a good excuse to drink during the day. I made sure we hosted a lot of bridge, so Dick wouldn't have as much opportunity to nag at me so much. That plan backfired, however, when my husband accused me of flirting with the other men, and even cheating on him.

Of course, I would never do such a thing, but he was convinced. I hated to see my husband hurting so much. I did everything in my power to make Dick see that I loved him and no one else.

It was mid-afternoon Sunday when the train finally pulled into Portland's Union Station. My brother Tom was there with Daddy's car to take me to Mother's. His big hug soothed me, and his deep voice was reassuring as he filled me in on the arrangements. A few blocks away from the house, he interrupted himself.

"Bessian?"

Mother and Dad called me Bess. Everyone else called me Beth, which was short for Lydia Bethalee. I was named for our grandma, but I loved it when Tom used his pet name for me. When we were little, he just shortened my middle name, Bethalee, to Bess or Bessie. When the little neighbor girl would come around to call on my sister and me, she'd knock on the door and ask, "Can Bessie an' Luella come out to play?"

Tom's voice would rise to a high pitch as he mimicked her, "Bessian. Luella. Time to go play outside."

"How would you like to stop off at this little bistro that happens to serve liquor? You know Mother doesn't keep any at the house."

I breathed a sigh of relief.

"That would be great, Tom."

He handed me a cigarette and held his lighter for me. I felt better already.

Dad's funeral was on a beautiful September Monday, unusually warm for Portland. I was so numb, I don't remember too much about it. I was just relieved when it was over. Mother rode home with Roy and Luella, so Tom and I stopped off at the neighborhood bar again before going to Mother's to face a houseful of people.

When we arrived, I saw that my best friend, Jean, and her husband Joe had beat us back to the house after the service. I was happy to catch up with them, and they insisted I come over to visit with them while I was there. I wanted to spend as much time as I could with Mother, but by the end of the week, I was ready to get out and see some friends.

I drove Dad's car the short distance from 70th Street to Yamhill Drive, and Jean and I went immediately out her back door and took a walk around lush green Mount Tabor. Dick and I had some happy years there with good neighbors and good friends before we went east for Dick's job. He didn't like Joe as well as some of our other friends. He thought he drank too much, and he didn't like the attention he paid me. So I was happy to have the chance to be with my friends without worrying about keeping Dick entertained and happy.

By the time Jean and Joe's kids, Sonny and Karen, got home from school, Jean and I had been playing cribbage and catching up with each other all day. Just like the good old days, we talked and snacked on Jean's buttery Chex mix and her famous peanut brittle as we played, so we weren't hungry for lunch.

"Karen, Sonny! Aren't you a sight for sore eyes," I greeted them as they came in and kissed their mother and then me on our cheeks.

"Oh, it's so good to see you! How's Nancy, how's Jim?" Karen asked.

"They are doing well. Happy in school, well Nancy is anyway. She sends her love to you all. She misses you so, Karen."

Our daughters were inseparable, just like Jean and I had always been, so it was very hard for Nancy to move away and have to make new friends.

When Joe got home, he started making dinner immediately after he freshened our cocktails for us and made one for himself. He set the first drink down by Jean, "My lovely wife," and then he set mine down next to me, "My polka-dotted beauty!"

Joe and I had an unspoken chemistry between us and a mutual appreciation club. I allowed him to flirt with me, and on occasion I might reply in kind—when Dick was out of hearing range. But I was never alone with him. I made sure Jean or someone else was always there. He might have pursued an affair with me, but I was not that kind of woman; besides, my affection for Jean, not to mention my respect for my husband, would never allow me to consider such a betrayal.

Joe was a salesman by vocation, but besides being a charmer with his clients and with the ladies, he was also an untrained gourmet chef. He could have owned or worked in any of the top-rated restaurants that Dick and I had ever eaten in, based on flavor alone, not to mention his presentation. I learned all my best culinary tricks from him. Mother taught me the basics, but Joe's techniques were the cherry on top of my cooking.

Over the years, it got so I could throw a meal together without looking at a recipe, even when Dick unexpectedly brought company home from work. I quickly earned a reputation among Dick's bosses and colleagues, and my meals became a secret sales weapon with clients old and new. I learned early that I was to prepare for more mouths than I expected, and when no one joined our family for dinner, the kids and I often ate leftovers for lunch.

Dick wasn't one to enjoy leftovers too often, so on the weekends, I would make him a pork chop or a steak, while the kids and I finished whatever was in the refrigerator to make room for a new week's worth of food. I went shopping every Monday morning, armed with a list and coupons. I found the best deals I could to make our money stretch. Dick still said that I spent too much, although he insisted on keeping his membership at the tennis club. Our compromise was buying the moderately-priced cigarettes rather than the bargain-priced ones. Neither of us could stand the taste of the lower-priced brands.

Besides my parents and my brother, Jean and Joe were the people who I was the most myself with. They were so easy-going, like me. When Joe did anything, he didn't get anxious, agitated, or angry when things didn't go as planned, unlike my husband, who blew a gasket if things didn't go his way. I learned to stay quiet and to stay out of Dick's way when he got like that. Joe just laughed about it and cleaned up the mess.

It also helped that Joe could mix the best drinks. Jean and Joe's annual holiday party was always THE party of the season. No one ever missed it because everyone knew that holiday cheer would be found there. The hosts served only the finest liquors, had the tastiest food, and told the funniest stories.

Before we moved away, Dick and I never partook of the drinks at those parties, since we just weren't interested in drinking liquor then, but these many years later during this time of mourning and of re-union, I didn't say no.

After a couple of Joe's cocktails, Jean and I weren't feeling any pain, and we laughed until our bellies hurt as he entertained us with his observations on life and odd happenings with his clients while we patiently waited for dinner.

When Joe learned that I'd taken the train up for Dad's funeral, he just shook his head.

"It's all right, Joe. The airline ticket was just too expensive, and I got to see some pretty views from my seat."

"That Dick is a cheap son of a bitch, isn't he?"

"No. I didn't want to spend the money on a plane ticket. Really, Joe, it's OK. I am in no hurry. I got here in time for the funeral, and that's all that matters."

"Well, he got you in a sleeper car at least?"

I looked at Joe, but I didn't respond, except to say, "At least it wasn't a bus ticket."

"Damn!" Joe just shook his head at me and looked at Jean as he said, "I'm going to get you a plane ticket home, Beth, and that's all there is to it."

"Oh, no, please don't, Joe." I looked at Jean, hoping she would step in for me. Dick would be so angry if I came home on a plane.

He didn't want to be shown up by another man, especially by Joe, and especially when it came to me. I'd be in for it if I didn't come home on the train ticket he'd bought. Jean saw my expression and suggested to her husband that maybe I wanted to have the time alone on the train. I nodded in agreement.

It was true. Although the train is not the most comfortable mode of travel, I was looking forward to the idle time. Mother had already been stockpiling crossword puzzles for my return trip, and Tom gave me his favorite deck of cards before he left to get back to his job in San Francisco, where he reported the news on the NBC television station.

"They give 'em away for free on the airplane, Bessian! I'll get a fresh deck on my way home."

"I don't know." Joe looked from Jean to me, and somehow understood our silent communication.

"It doesn't feel right, Beth."

Joe wanted to cash in my train ticket, and he'd pay the difference for a plane ticket, but he gave in when I told him I was leaving in just a couple of days anyway and I didn't want him to go to the trouble. Finally, Joe let it go, with a frown and more shaking of his head, and I was relieved.

I just wanted peace with my husband, and for some time, there had not been much peace at all.

Lydia

I KNEW IT WOULD BE

I was awake before the sun rose high enough in the sky to shine into the bedroom. I couldn't hear anyone stirring yet, but I arose and got dressed. I pulled the covers up on my bed and made sure the room was tidy before I went into the kitchen to wait for Dutch's family to join me.

The distance to my home wasn't so great, yet it would be a long journey today. My heart was heavy with dread, particularly in light of the reception I had from my brother-in-law Fred's ex-wife, Youtha, the day before at Mama's surprise birthday party. I feared the reception I imagined I would get from my family I had abandoned two years before.

"Morning!" my sister came into the room and started to get break-fast together.

"Need help?" I asked half-heartedly.

"No thank you. I got my routine."

Dutch's husband, Tom, had purchased a train ticket for me to get home. Three hours down the rails, judgment day awaited me. I was being forced to face Oliver, my husband. I was being forced to face my children. Would he allow me back into the house? Would I be allowed back into his bed? Did I even want to return? I thought I had made the choice to be free when I left with Isaac, but I had just saddled myself to another man who expected me to serve him.

What did I want now? What did I really want? Isaac taught me to ask that question when no one else ever bothered to ask me. I never even bothered to ask myself that question before now. Did I really want to go home?

No one knew I was coming. They wouldn't miss me if I just stayed on the train and kept going. Denver was a stop on this line. Perhaps Denver would hold some opportunity for me. I could open a business. Perhaps I could have a laundry service for the miners or run a boarding house for independent single ladies. Not a house of ill-repute, but a home for women like me, who just wanted to be free. I could open a cafe for the government workers in the capital.

Traveling with Isaac Ziglar had opened my eyes to a whole world of other possibilities. He told me about people he had met and what their enterprises were. When we were in towns, I observed what establishments were in operation and who was running them. There were more ways to make a living than farming or running a mercantile or a teamster service, even for a single woman.

I would be anonymous in a big city. No one would know me, nor would they have to. I could restart my life.

"You're awfully quiet, Lydia. What are you up to?"

Dutch looked at me suspiciously as she brought my breakfast to the table. How did she know me so well? I didn't respond to her question.

"Thanks for the eggs, Dutch. They are fresh from this morning, aren't they?"

Not answering me, she carried two steaming mugs of black coffee to the table and placed one in front of me and set the other at her place. She brought a plate of lightly browned toast and the butter dish and set them between us next to the bright orange jar of marmalade.

"I'm glad you stopped by here on your way home, Lydia. It's been good to be with you."

I thought I noted a hint of sarcasm in her voice, but she reached across and touched my hand to let me know she really meant it.

Tom got up a few minutes later and came into the kitchen pulling his braces up over his shoulders so his pants wouldn't fall down around his ankles when he walked. Reaching for a triangle of toast, he said, "I'll just have my coffee and we'll get you to the station, Lydia."

"I'm ready."

The way Dutch looked at me, I could tell she didn't believe me. In fact, I wasn't sure I was ready.

I could just keep going. I didn't have to get off in Seward. I had pocketed some change here and there as Isaac and I traveled, so I actually had enough to get me to Denver and last for a week or so. That should be enough time to find a job to pay my way until I could get a business going.

"Your children are going to be real happy to see you, sister."

My children. Dutch would never have left her children, and I knew she just said that to remind me that I still had motherly duties I should be attending to. She was right, of course.

After breakfast, Tom got me to the train on time. I only had the one piece of luggage. It was not too burdensome to carry it myself as I traveled alone.

The morning trip back to Nebraska was not anything like our journey west when Oliver and I were young and newlywed. I had plenty of time to remember how we brought our furniture to be transported on the train with us, along with our luggage. And of course, our baby's things. Oh, what a train ride that was! I barely sat down at all the entire ride unless our boy was asleep.

James was two and into everything. He went up and down the aisle making new friends at every seat. He inspected people's shoes and their food. The way he begged for food, you would think we never fed him. I was embarrassed, but no one seemed to mind. They shared a bit with him without hesitation; a piece of apple here, a slice of cheese there.

By the time we pulled out our own meal, James was not hungry anymore. But then he slept. He climbed onto the seat between Oliver and me. Oliver pulled him back so that his little boots barely reached the edge of the eat. As he leaned into me, I could feel his warm body slump into sleep as the train rocked us back and forth. I dared not make a move lest he awaken and start to whine and cry as he did when he was too tired to wake up, but too awake to go back to sleep. I kept my arm around him to ensure he would not fall forward and knock his head on the wooden floor of the train car.

Like his grandson, Oliver's father had a hard time sitting in one place for long, and he, too, took to walking the aisle of the train. He went farther, though, into other cars, meeting nearly everyone we traveled with.

Now, 20 years later, the train was the same and the speed was the same, but on this journey, I was alone. Alone with my thoughts, I tried to come up with some excuse for my absence—for my infidelity. I didn't only betray my husband and my children, I also betrayed myself. My middle name is Fidelia, for my father's sister. It means faithful and loyal, but I couldn't even live up to my own name. How would Oliver receive me? What would the children say? How could I ever explain?

Some people slept through the morning, rocked to sleep as the train rambled across the still-wide-open spaces heading west. My mind was full of home. I was getting excited even though I feared what they would say when they saw me. Would they be resistant to my returning.

I watched the light change on the landscape as the sun rose higher in the sky from behind us, I could see the rolling grassy hills and the trees clearly. Dutch gave me a quilt for the trip, and I felt wrapped in Mama's love since her hands had stitched it together. It would be a warm day, and I took Mama's quilt off my lap and folded it neatly.

I had left everything behind when I went away with Isaac Ziglar. All I had was a change of clothes in my valise. The same dress I had on now was the dress I wore when I climbed into his rig for the first time to leave my life behind. I'd be home about the same time as the family would be getting home from the fields and from school. I would try to get home quick enough to get supper started.

The other passengers were restless, and some moved about. Some went to the diner car, and others went to the lavatories to freshen up. A few men went outside and stood in the open back end of the train car to smoke their pipes and take in the fresh air.

I just stayed put. There was nothing I needed to do. Even after my sleepless night listening to Tom and Dutch snoring on the other side of the bedroom wall, a peace had descended upon me. I considered it to be grace. What would be would be.

No time seemed to have passed at all before the train pulled into the station just before our home station at Seward. I didn't recognize anyone who got off or anyone waiting outside to meet them. No one would be meeting me at the station. I'd have to get a ride out from town to our place in Goehner. Then I realized there would be prying eyes and questions.

People would recognize me and ask where I'd been for two years. I suddenly realized that my response didn't need to be detailed or complicated. I would tell a partial truth and just say that I'm coming from my sister's. That's all that needed to be said... if I even got off there.

It was time to make a decision. Stay on the train, or go home? It was my choice to make and mine alone. There was no one to make that choice for me, and no one to take that choice from me this time.

Even though we had been sitting so close to one another, the woman who had been my seat companion and I hadn't spoken the whole ride out. She was reading her Bible and I felt a pang of guilt as I realized I had not read my Bible in a few years. I had left our church when Gracie died three years before.

I was angry at God, and I didn't believe His Word was meant for me. My Gracie was my last baby, my last girl. It was like she was my other two babies who died, all rolled into one. Sure, I had my two other daughters, Vinnie and Belle, but I suppose I took them for granted now, even though I should maybe know better.

Little Grace's passing was too much for me. I was too hurt to understand God's mercy. I didn't feel any of it then. I felt like God was dead, too. How could He have taken my third baby from me? She was precocious and sweet. Her angel face could be so pure and innocent, even when she knew she was being defiant and naughty. And so smart. Grace was already in the first reader at school even though she was only five. Then the fever came and took her from us.

The Bible-reading woman and I both looked out the window as the train pulled out of the station. One hour until I'd reach Seward. To take my mind off my bitter heartache, I searched for something new to look at outside the moving train.

We were passing an abandoned, dilapidated farmhouse. The weather-beaten siding was faded and gray, and the shutters were hanging on a slant by one nail. The roof was caving in where the weight of winter snow had challenged the strength of the builder's skills. That house reminded me of something I couldn't quite put my finger on.

Needless to say, my family had gone without peddler's wares for a couple of years. The children would need shoes. I wondered if Lee would be at home. Two years older now, he may be about ready to leave home and make his way in the world. Dutch had not told me anything about my children. I hadn't even asked.

She said that her Josie was in Montana teaching for the summer. Dutch missed her daughter so, and I sympathized with her, but felt pride in my niece that she would have the courage to go so far away from home to the wilds of Montana and take a job. What must that be like, to earn your own money?

Aside from selling some eggs and milk to passing travelers, and occasionally at the mercantile when I'd make the rare journey into town to get a good price for my butter, I'd never earned my own money before. How liberating it would be to not rely on anyone for the most basic needs. I had pocketed any spare change that came my way, and over two years, I'd saved a little bit, enough to have a taste of self-sufficiency should the need ever arise.

I had always depended on someone else: my father, my husband, Mr. Ziglar. My brother-in-law Tom had even bought me this train ticket. Josie had taught and brought the money home to her parents for years, but she must have been tired of feeling obliged to her parents, so off she went to make her own way.

Josie was a smart girl, and she enjoyed reading nearly more than anyone I'd ever met besides Mr. Ziglar. She would recite snippets of poems and write a few lines of verse that came to her from goodness knows where.

Josie's cousin and my niece Goldie, Amy and Ol's daughter, was teaching in Montana already. Dutch said that when Goldie let Josie know about the shortage of teachers and opportunity for more pay than in Iowa, Josie set out on an adventure.

I envied her even though Josie was a little old to not be married. She was close to 35 already! What would she do without a husband? Perish the thought.

I felt a flash of gratitude for my husband, and then guilt for having treated him so poorly by leaving him for another man. I was far from worthy. I was so flawed that I didn't deserve him, although it helped me to remember that he was not perfect either. The story of Oliver's imperfections can be told another time.

It occurred to me that my home may not be my home anymore. Inasmuch as I felt my husband was a stranger to me, I must also have felt like a stranger to him. Would he have me back? I felt certain he would. He just couldn't reject me.

The level of fear rose in my heart as I realized that just as I'd forsaken him for someone else, he very well may have moved on to someone else as well. Oh, I hoped that wasn't the case. I began to long to be home with him again. I wondered about the children. What had I missed in two years?

My silent and anonymous companion on this train journey shut the Bible she had been reading since she got on the train and settled in across from me. She rested her hand on the cover and sighed as she looked up and into my face. She said, "It's all gonna be all right, isn't it?"

Her face relaxed into an expression of relief, and in that moment, I knew it would be. I didn't ask what she was relieved about, but in my mind, I thanked her for her reassurance. The message of encouragement she took for herself from whatever she had read, I took to be for me, too. I smiled at her and nodded.

"Yes, I think it will be."

I made my decision in that moment.

In 1916, the same year that my grandchild, Lee and Josie's little Elsie, went to be with the angels, Oliver's older sister Dora died, leaving my brother Hi alone with their children. I realized then that one must come to terms with death. It is all around us, yet it does not dominate our lives for long.

Death should bring the whole world to a complete stop, but it does not. It is devastating, but in time, we learn that life goes on. That's what I learned anyway.

If I could have stopped the world, I would have, for myself and Oliver, for Josie and Lee, for Hi. But the reality is that the earth continues to turn. I remember asking to myself how could people go about their daily tasks, and laugh about silly things, and complain about even sillier things when there is grief all around them?

My eyes had been opened to it, and I regarded people differently now. Their faces may be happy, but what do their eyes express from their deepest hearts, and from their truths of sorrow, grief, and of loss?

I resented people who seemed to be unaware of my loss. I'd think, *Don't you realize I am in pain?* Then it crossed my mind that even if they were aware of my pain, they may not be able to empathize with it, just as I cannot always know or even care about another person's pain.

As the world keeps turning, it winds up the grief and the pain, just as thread is wound on a spool. Occasionally, it suddenly unwinds, and like a tornado can come up suddenly and take me up into a deep, dark, stormy sky for a time. It is impossible to get my footing, and I feel so far from safety and calm that I think it will never end, but eventually I return to the solid ground. I come to spend more and more time there than in the gusty storm that carries and twists me around in its merciless currents like a rag doll.

I felt the return of the big storms with my grandbaby's death and then Dora's just a couple of months later. Then the silver lining was revealed to me. From my own experience with the pain from losing the most precious things God would ever let me have, for a time, I knew how to spot that same pain in Lee and Josie even after their little Thomas came to liven their home again with his big personality and his long laughter.

I was able to provide comfort and understanding in a way that my sister Dutch couldn't even give to her own daughter. Dutch had never lost her own baby, so when she went to care for Josie in Havelock in the weeks after baby Elsie left us, she was impatient for Josie to be up and dressed. In a way, it was good. It had been a few weeks since the funeral, and while Josie was a strong girl, I truly believed that a broken heart could kill someone.

When a horse is down, you have to get it up and walking immediately, or you may lose it. If Josie had stayed in bed, we may have lost her. She had no reason to get up like I'd had. My sons demanded my survival so they could live. Elsie was Josie's first baby, and the only remedy for her broken heart would be to have another.

Eventually, life did go on, as it does, and Lee and Josie's family did grow until they were five in all. Thomas was joined by darling Cynthia Luella who had Elsie and Josie's beautiful blue eyes, and then by Lydia Bethalee. I was so pleased when they named her for me. She was my favorite, and she was bright and shiny like a new penny, with her fiery red hair and freckles, which I told her were angel kisses, all over her pudgy little body. From the day she was born, Lee called her Bess, but Josie wanted to call her Bethalee, so that's what I called her, too.

Not long after Bethalee was born, Lee's fascination and mechanical experience with automobiles paid off and he got a wonderful job in an auto shop. That's when Lee and Josie moved their family out to Portland, Oregon.

As the second world war was beginning, the Kaiser Industrial Company opened up some shipyards on the west coast, and they employed Lee as a Yard Maintenance Superintendent, whatever that meant. He was paid well, and he was pleased to have the new position. I was so proud of my son. He had persevered through hardships and came out on the other side alive and well.

When I came home in 1915, I missed our Lee when I realized he wasn't home anymore. During the summer, we got a postcard from him telling us he was doing well, but no word on when he'd be coming back.

We also got a letter from Dutch. She was very concerned about her Josie. She resented it that Tom had allowed my niece to go to Montana for a teaching job that paid better than any school did in Iowa. My sister told us she'd begged Josie to come home, and she thought maybe our Lee and Josie were spending time together. That's what Amy had written her anyway. I thought that would be nice for them, since they were both so far from home. They had made good friends there, but there's nothing like family when it comes to being so far from home. I knew.

I was lucky that our brothers and sisters had moved with us when my father-in-law, Peter Franklin, brought us west in 1885. It was a comfort to have them join us for the journey and help us get settled in, especially when my second baby came for a brief year before she left us again.

It wasn't long before we got word from Lee and Josie themselves. They had gone to Colorado when summer was done, and they'd gotten married. To each other. I was shocked. I wondered how my sister was taking it, but I didn't want to actually write out the question in a letter to her.

Josie was a good twelve years older than our Lee. He was the handsomest of our boys. He could have had any of the pretty girls who seemed to smile bigger and shine brighter every time he came around. He chose his spinster cousin. Much as I loved my niece, I didn't understand why, but I knew enough not to question. I had also made choices in my life that didn't make sense to anyone but me. I'd had to come to terms with that and forgive myself, but it also meant I could not judge others for their choices.

Josie was a sweet girl, but she knew her own mind, and she could be quite a talker once she got started. She was headstrong and determined, and I suppose she had made her mind up about our Lee. She was getting on in years, after all. He was only 22, but she was 34 already. I wondered if there might be something else going on. I would never tell anyone, but I counted the months from the time they were married until she had her baby, and it was exactly ten. So they hadn't had to marry. I guessed they truly loved each other.

Once they moved back home to Nebraska, I saw that they were very attached to one another. They were initially very shy, not standing close or touching one another in our presence. They seemed very aware that we might be judging them. They also did not announce to any of the neighbors that their mothers were sisters, so we didn't mention it to anyone either. The community knew our family, however, so it did get out. I was relieved that it didn't seem to hurt their standing in the community. Or ours.

Marrying one's cousin was not something unheard of. Mama said we had relations going back who were first cousins. In Pa's family, there were cousins who had married going back some generations, so I knew it was not a unique occurrence, but it was not so much the fashion anymore like it once was. In fact, I knew it was against the law in many states. Colorado was one state that still allowed cousin marriages. Nebraska did not, but it did respect a marriage that had been solemnized in another state, so they were safe to live there.

Lee and Josie were sweet together. She made a nice little home in Havelock, just south of Lincoln and halfway between Winterset and Seward by train. Somehow, he found a job as a machinist assistant in town not too far from their new home.

Lee had only gone up to the sixth grade and didn't enjoy books so much. He was always an active boy who enjoyed being outside with his brothers and working the land with his father. He especially loved it when something broke down and he got to help fix it. Then there came a day when Oliver couldn't fix it, but Lee managed to.

Not that Lee was ever in competition with his father, but he felt so proud that he could do something his Papa couldn't. Then his chest really swelled when Oliver praised him over it. He didn't go overboard with praise, so when Oliver talked well about something someone did, it meant all that much more.

That was the beginning of Lee's work using his hands as well as his brain to operate, fix, and even design machinery.

I was over the moon when their baby was born. Elsie Alberta was a sweet little thing. She looked like her father, just like my Lee had looked when he was born with a long body and long fingers, taking more after Oliver's side of the family than mine. But her coloring was like my mama's—pale skin and light hair. Although babies' eyes are usually blue when they are born, I knew this baby's eyes would stay blue.

Dutch brought her youngest daughter Edith for a visit, and when Lee and Josie took them on a ride out to see us, we took pictures. Elsie's Aunt Edith put Elsie's first pair of shoes on her little feet, compliments of Aunt Ethel, who had to stay home in Iowa with her own baby.

Then one early October morning, Lee came and told us their little Else had died. He said that they were taking a ride and she was in Josie's arms the whole time. When they got home, Josie realized that she wasn't breathing. She tried to rouse her, but her little soul had gone to heaven.

Oliver went right out and bought a family plot in the cemetery up the road from our farm, and we buried her there. I went to Havelock to stay for a week so Josie could stay in bed just as long as she needed to, as I'd done all those years ago when my first little girl, Jessie, died.

Oliver's sister, Mary, had cared for me and for James so I could sleep and sleep and sleep, escaping the reality that my child was in the ground. Lee had his job to return to, and Josie was alone in their little house during the day. Although their Aunt Dora's health was not very good, she was still faithful and went over to keep Lee and Josie's house in order and make sure they stayed fed until Dutch could come to stay with them.

I had stayed with them for as long as I could. Oliver seemed anxious about me being away. He didn't say as much, but I got the impression he was concerned I'd run off on him again. I thought it best to get home and ease his mind. I took the train home to Seward. It was a short trip, but it was just enough time to reflect on how far Oliver and I had come from the day I first returned home to him.

I thought back to the pain we all felt the day I first came back home. When he left me alone in the kitchen after supper, I didn't know what to do. In my mind's eye, I could see the shadows lengthen in the room as the time passed and the sun sank lower on the horizon. I watched its progress out the west window, and just sat at the old wooden kitchen table like a stone statue. My mind was a blank. It was empty of everything. I was empty.

Belle had gone to the neighbors' to give us some privacy, and when she came back after a time, she silently lit the lamps and heated the water to finish the dishes.

"The neighbors have a new calf," she informed me as if it was just a regular day, as if I hadn't just returned after two years during which time I lived in sin with another man and barely gave my family a second thought. She didn't look at me though.

"Oh, that's nice, dear."

I was suddenly so tired I could barely keep my eyes open.

"I think I will go to sleep now."

Belle stood at the screen door and looked out toward the barn.

"You want me to get the boys to come in and get ready for bed, Mama?"

"Yes, dear, thank you. Good night."

"Good night, Mama."

She didn't turn around to face me, and although she seemed to have accepted my return, I felt she still didn't want me to touch her, so I kept my distance.

"Sleep tight."

"I will, Mama."

I eased quietly into the bedroom, turning the handle carefully so as not to awaken Oliver. I had taken my bag in when I first got home, unpacked my few clothes, and hung them on the nail on the wall next to the chest of drawers Oliver had made for me after we got married. It was the biggest piece of furniture we had to move with us from Iowa.

I opened the top drawer and pulled out a nightie. I felt a tug at my heart when I realized that my things were just as I left them. Oliver had not touched a thing in those two years, as if he expected me back at any time. I slipped the white flannel gown over my head and eased my dress down to the floor. I hung it up with my other dress. I pulled the brush through my long hair 100 times, counting silently as I did each and every night.

I didn't hear Oliver breathing, so I knew he was still awake. His back was to me, and he was facing the window. The moon had risen, and it lit up the room through the branches of the tree that stood guard right outside. I didn't need to worry about waking him, but I did worry about how he would receive me back into our marital bed after I had shattered his heart with the news that I had been unfaithful with our peddler. I felt deep remorse in the pit of my stomach. It hurt, and I knew I must just bear the pain of it.

I sat slowly on the edge of the bed, and eased back to lie down, facing the ceiling. I didn't reach for my husband, and he stayed on his side. Our bodies barely touched, and he did nothing to bring us closer together. Neither one of us slept all night. Our silence was loud. I couldn't break it, though, and neither did he. I'd already asked for his forgiveness. There was nothing else I could say to make it better, and anything else I said would make his pain that much worse, so I kept quiet, and so did he.

Laying there, unable to relax and unable to sleep, I thought about our first evening back together as a family gathered around the kitchen table. We all sat in uncomfortable silence while my sons and husband ate. Belle and I looked at our hands folded on our laps. Anxious about my place in the family, I was too sick to my stomach to say anything.

As they were finishing up, Belle got up and started washing dishes.

"Boys, you go out and take care of the cows now," Oliver said.

"All right, Papa," they said in unison before pushing their chairs back from the table and shoving open the screen to leap off the porch and race to the barn.

Belle looked at each of us then and must have sensed our need for privacy. She put some squash that was laying on the counter in a basket and went to the door.

"Papa, I'm going to run to the neighbors with some extra squash I picked this morning before I left for work."

"Thank you, Belle. You're a good girl."

We were alone. It was so painfully awkward between us that I started to get up to finish the dishes, and Oliver quietly said, "Sit down, Lydia."

I complied. I didn't want to have this conversation, but I knew I had to before we went to our shared bed together.

"Explain yourself, please," he said.

I looked at him, at a loss for words even though I had practiced in my head all day what I would say to him. All I could say was, "I'm sorry, Oliver. Please forgive me."

"For what?"

"For leaving you and the children."

"What do I need to know, Lydia?"

How should I answer this question? How much did he really want to know? How much did I really want him to know? I didn't know where to begin.

"What did I do wrong?"

I looked up at his face, surprised by his question. To my horror, he began to cry. I'd never seen my husband cry. Even when our babies died, he did his crying alone, or in the dark when I couldn't see him; I could only feel his body shake in the bed next to me as my own body shook with my tears. He held me and my hair would be wet with his tears, but we never even looked each other in the eye when we were going through it. We never voiced our deepest sorrows to one another.

I felt tears running down my face now, and I quickly wiped them away. My voice would have failed me, so I didn't answer him for a moment. I only shook my head. When he looked down at the table, I got up and sat next to him. Taking a deep breath, I put my hands over his and assured him, "You did nothing wrong, Ollie. I had to go, is all."

"I know that's what you said, but why? I didn't know you were not happy here with me. Is that why you left, because you were unhappy with me?"

His eyes searched my face for an answer. I had already had a similar conversation with Dutch, and the practice made it easier to just say it to my husband.

"I wanted to escape for a bit, Oliver."

"Escape? Escape what, Lydia? I haven't shackled you. I never mistreated you. I never even looked at another woman, Lydia."

"I know, Oliver."

I felt relieved when he looked away from me again. His head was bowed down as his gaze fixed upon our hands resting together on the tabletop. We sat for a few more minutes in silence, and my mind got quiet. I took another deep breath.

"I was so sad when Grace died. I felt so alone, Oliver. I missed all three of our little girls so much; I had to get away from here. I don't know why. I can't explain it."

"I know it, Lydia. I miss them, too, I hurt, too."

He lifted his face to look into mine, and as my eyes met his, I could see his face reddening. His voice rose in pitch and volume as he continued, "But you left me alone. I was so lonely these past two years, Lydia. I did my best with the children, and Belle was so good to stay and take care of us."

His voice trailed off then, and after a long pause, I asked the question that had bothered me since I got on the train this morning.

"Will you let me come home, Oliver? Can I stay?"

"Why couldn't you, Lydia? This is your home, your family."

I looked away from him. My eyes closed as I remembered Isaac's lips on mine, his hands holding my body close to his; the ecstasy of our naked bodies moving together under a wide black sky lit only by the Milky Way, caressed by a warm summer breeze.

I felt my face get red. Oliver took his hands out from under mine and stood up. I opened my eyes to see him back away from the table, away from me.

"Why couldn't you, Lydia?"

He asked again, but I could tell he knew why from the look on his face. His eyes were open wide. He looked horrified, as if he'd seen my memory with his own eyes. He repeated the question a little louder, "Why couldn't you?"

I just looked at him and shook my head. I didn't have to answer him. He already knew.

"Ziglar?"

I nodded my head slowly.

Oliver's face crumpled and his shoulders sagged. He let out a wail the likes of which I'd never heard, and he backed farther away from me, turned on his heel, and strode to the door that led to our bedroom. He slammed the door behind him so hard that the house shook.

Tears ran down the sides of my face and wet the pillow thinking of the way my husband had come home just hours before, not anticipating me and my confession. My heart hurt thinking of the quiet reception I'd met and then the pain I'd brought to him.

Oliver had knocked his boots against the steps as he kicked the dirt and mud off them before coming into the kitchen. I realized my heart was beating out of my chest and my knees were so weak that I didn't trust them to support my weight, so I gripped the back of the chair as I waited for him to come in.

"Sure smells good in here, Belle!" is what he said as he swung the screen wide. And then he stopped in the doorway when he saw me. His eyes opened wide, and he didn't seem able to speak for a few seconds.

"Look who's home, Papa!" said Billy enthusiastically.

"She's been at Aunt Dutch's," added Stubb.

"Yes, yes," Oliver said simply.

He just looked at me. He exhaled, looked away, and walked to the sink, where he washed his hands for a few minutes. I didn't remember him ever taking as long to clean up for dinner, especially when he'd been working hard in the fields all day. He would be so hungry, he said that his guts felt like they were eating themselves.

I always made sure his meal was hot and on the table when he walked in the door, so he'd never have to wait. Until I didn't. Until I rode off with Mr. Ziglar and the stove was cold and the cows were un-milked, leaving only a note.

"I have to go," was all I could manage to write. Four words. No explanation. I wouldn't have gone if I'd had to come up with an excuse, an explanation. I would have talked myself out of it, talked myself out of an adventure, an affair, which I just had to experience. At the time, there was no saying no to it. I don't know why.

If any other woman in our community had done such a thing, my tongue would have been worn out talking about it, judging her. Such a harsh judge I would have been against someone else, but for me, what I did just made sense. I wouldn't expect anyone to understand.

As he shut off the faucet, I said meekly, "Hello, Oliver."

He turned around with a dishtowel in his hands and leaned against the sink. He just looked at me like he couldn't believe his eyes.

"Where have you been, Lydia?" His voice was calm, although I could see in his eyes there was a storm brewing deep inside him.

We rarely had ever been cross with one another, but when we were, he would get even quieter than usual, and his deep voice would get deeper. I felt he was trying to soothe me, since I tended to talk fast and yell some. I didn't like that. I didn't like him trying to tell me how to be. Like how I was being was unacceptable.

When I was mad, I wanted to be mad. I didn't want to talk calmly in a lady-like voice. I wanted to let it out and express how I felt like distant booming thunder and crackling lightening, even if I didn't always know how I felt.

"At Dutch's."

It wasn't a total lie. I was just coming home from her place.

"Iowa, eh?" he sat down at the head of the table and put some chicken and bread on his plate. He always ate his salad last. He said it helped settle the rest of the meal in his stomach.

"How are the folks in Iowa?"

"They are doing good. They say hello."

It was quiet at the table. Belle had taken her seat next to her father, and sat quietly, not taking any food onto her plate as the boys and their father ate. Oliver took a bite of chicken and wiped his chin with his other hand, as usual. I was comforted by the familiarity of seeing my family at the table. I joined them, sitting across from Oliver.

"When is Lee getting home?" I asked, looking at the empty place setting.

"He's in Montana, Mama," Stubb told me.

I looked to Oliver and Belle for confirmation. "Montana? Why? What's he doing there?"

"Doing some logging up north," Oliver told me. He didn't look at me.

I didn't understand the connection between my son and logging. "Why?"

"He wanted to make some money," Belle said. "I think he wanted to get out of here for a while. Surely you could understand that." Her voice was cold, and she looked away from me.

Oliver seemed to want to provide me with a gentler response and said softly, "It was a new opportunity for him. Baseball didn't work out so well for him."

"Baseball?" I never thought of that as any more than a fun pastime for any of our boys.

"First, he played for the Collegians, Mama, and last year he played for the Prohibitionists!" Stubb told me. "He was a pitcher. Pitched 21 straight innings one game! All the other boys were injured, and he just kept throwing that ball! It was a long game. They kept getting tied up!"

Oliver added, "He enjoyed it, but he was pretty low in the league rankings, so they didn't have him back. He headed up to Montana instead."

"You let him go?"

Oliver stopped chewing and looked up from his plate at me. He didn't respond. Then he took a bite of cornbread and chewed it slowly, his eyes never leaving my face. I didn't know what to say. Feeling foolish, I looked away from him.

"You gonna eat, Mama?"

"No, Billy. I'm not hungry."

I had been very hungry when the train pulled into Seward that afternoon, but food was the last thing on my mind. I was concerned about who I might run into there, but I needed to get home somehow. I would have to ask someone for a ride.

I recognized our neighbor, Mr. Schultz, near the train station and asked if he might drop me off at home. He agreed and was polite enough to ask me no questions as we rode silently out from town. Mr.

Schultz stopped his wagon in front of my house to let me off before continuing down the road to his place, fifteen minutes further along.

The place seemed cold and lonely. The house looked the same, yet the porch needed to be swept. Oliver's fields looked like they had the day I rode away with the traveling man, ready to be planted. The garden was smaller than usual, and it needed to be weeded.

No one was home, but old Shep came walking around the corner of the house. He stopped when he saw me, and when he realized who I was, he came bounding over to me, like he did when he was a puppy. His tongue was hanging out, and it looked like he had a smile on his face. He nearly knocked me over as he circled me and got in as close as he possibly could, but remembering his training, he didn't jump up on me. If he had done so, he'd have knocked me down. Shep was a big dog, and he had always helped keep the coyotes and foxes out of the hen house.

My tears fell on him as I petted his head, taking his soft ears in my hands. I almost kissed him as he welcomed me with no questions or judgment, only pure joy. That was a good greeting. I felt ready then to go inside and put on my apron. I'd see what we had for supper and put it together.

As I got the dishes and glasses out of the cupboard, my hands were shaking. There was a tingling sensation running down my arms into my fingers. I couldn't quite catch my breath, and a whole cloud of frenzied butterflies fluttered in my stomach. Who would be home first? Would they welcome me with hugs or send me away? How would I answer their questions?

I set the table for six as the chicken was frying on the stove and the cornbread baked in the oven. I picked some lettuce along with some handfuls of weeds and radishes. Doing these tasks had helped calm my nerves. I put the salad on the table and dished up the chicken just as I heard the children turn off the road onto our drive. They were singing a song I didn't recognize. Just short of the door, they stopped and wondered aloud about the smell of the cooking food.

"What is that?"

Stubb's voice had changed a bit. He didn't have a high baby voice anymore.

"Smells like dinner!"

Billy burst into the kitchen with my youngest son hard on his heels, and they both stopped dead in their tracks when they saw me standing there. Billy ran his hand over his head to take his hat off, uncovering his curly blond hair. It looked like they'd each grown a foot since I'd gone away. They looked at each other to make sure they weren't seeing an apparition, and then they burst into smiles.

"Mama!"

They ran to me, embracing me with such great force that they almost knocked me over. After brief hugs, I told them to get off me before I fell down.

"Mama, where have you been?"

"I came from your Aunt Dutch's in Iowa, boys. My train just got in this morning."

"I missed you, Mama."

"I missed you, too, Stubb. I missed you both."

Just then, Belle came in. She was startled to see me and looked from me to the table and back to me, taking me in, her eyes traveling from my head to my toes and back up to my face. There was no smile on her face, and a chill ran up the back of my neck.

"Look who's here, Belle!"

She nodded. "I see, Stubb. Hello, Mother."

Her greeting was flat. She was not happy to see me, and my heart sank, but I replied with as much strength and warmth in my voice as I could muster, "Hello, Belle. How have you been?"

"Just fine, thank you. You can see the garden is doing well."

My daughter was making an effort, but she was formal and stiff with me, like she would be with a stranger. That made my heart hurt.

"Yes, I got the lettuce and radishes for the salad out there."

"Thank you for getting dinner together for us. I was going to do that when I got home."

"I know, dearie, but I wanted it to be ready for you all when you got home. How was school today?"

"I'm not in school anymore, Mother. I am working at the mercantile now. I heard someone say they saw you get off the train earlier. I didn't know if I should believe them or not."

I wanted to touch my daughter, to hold her, but she didn't want me to. She seemed so angry. It was like I was a stranger who just came into her kitchen and took over. I guess that is just what I did do. But I didn't feel like a stranger; I was still their mother. It had been my kitchen after all, until I left.

"What has it been like, since I've been gone?"

Belle's eyes widened as if she was insulted by my question, and she looked at the boys. They had already sat down at the table and were picking at the corn bread when they thought I wasn't looking.

Instead of answering my question, Belle said, "Why don't you boys go ahead and eat before it gets cold. Papa will be here in a few minutes."

She turned her back to me to go the sink and wash her hands. Over her shoulder, she asked her brothers in a maternal tone, "Did you boys wash your hands?"

They had not, was what their dirty faces and impish grins told me.

"Get up and wash your hands! You know better than to sit at my table with dirty hands and faces!"

I was nervous as I said that. I tried not to allow my voice to shake. I had not been mothering them for two years. It was natural to me, but the way Belle looked at me, I was questioning myself. Judging myself. Who did I think I was, coming back here and thinking I could just take up my place again without doing some penance?

After the first night I came home, we never talked about it again. I never had to answer another question or give another explanation. I wanted to forget Mr. Ziglar as if I had never met him. And for the most part, I did. In time, the two years I spent away from my family dimmed from my memory. Things got back into a rhythm around the farm. I resumed my usual tasks, and I worked the garden back into shape. The children seemed happy, and even Belle warmed up to me again over time. I finally experienced contentment.

Contentment.

I didn't feel the ache of yearning for something else, of wanting more or new or different. I finally felt the peace of satisfaction. No matter what obstacles arose, or what losses I suffered, I knew that everything was going to be all right.

My life was good. I had enough of everything I needed. Soon after I settled back in at home, I realized I didn't need to be anyone other than who I was. I was enough.

It took months of sharing a bed before my husband would touch me. Then one night, he finally wrapped an arm around me as we went to sleep. The next night as we lay down, I turned my head to look into his eyes and I told him, "More than tongue can tell, Ollie."

He held me as close as ever, and then for me, it was like no time had passed, like I hadn't left him at all.

Acknowledgments

I would be remiss if I did not acknowledge the many people who helped me along this journey of becoming an author. There are enough names to fill a book, so even if you are not named below, if you have had a part in making this book bloom, you are included!

My mom, Nancy, wrote down the first story I ever dictated. Wonder what ever happened to it? It was about my three pet goldfish in their round glass bowl home, I believe. There may have been a cat cameo in it at some point. She read aloud to me. I say this because the next paragraph is about Dad reading with me, so I must mention here that she did, too. Dad did not write with me, however he did give excellent algebra and geometry instruction. This paragraph, now longer than Dad's, is really about Mom, and how she is ever my biggest fan and promoter. She sings my praises to anyone who will listen. It's embarrassing, really. May she never stop doing it.

My dad, Jerry, read books aloud with me, helping me to cement the syntax, plotlines, and rhythm of story in my brain and prime my creative pump. Our favorites were Alice in Wonderland and Through the Looking Glass, Mandy, and the entire Black Stallion series. I wanted to experience the world of Alec and the Black, so he took me to the

Golden Gate Fields racetrack in Albany to watch the ponies run. We even won some money!

Mrs. Nye was my 6th grade teacher who taught me not just how to write a story, but how to bind it with a cover! My first published work (my classmates and I got to read each other's stories) is a limited edition gathering dust on my bookshelf right now.

My English teacher and my professional mentor at Mt. Diablo High School, Mrs. Bergamini (although she insisted on me calling her Jan once I became a teacher, I was never comfortable doing it.) I have always respected her feedback and still use what I learned from her today. I am constantly on the lookout for redundancy. Oh, and Shakespeare! My life-long love affair with the Bard began in her class when we read Hamlet.

My Aunt Jo-Anne, whose career as a magazine editor and travel writer inspired me to write and to travel. Her generosity is unmatched, and the richest of her many gifts to me is her unconditional love and how she cherishes family bonds.

Teachers at Diablo Valley College like Clark McKowen who turned me on to funny physicists (that I knew who Richard P. Feynman was increased my popularity with physicists at cocktail parties) and other out of the box thinkers. Also, the one who taught me English Literature and Creative Writing in London and had the confidence in me to take on tutoring one of the blankest slates I've ever met. I regret to say that despite my best efforts and utmost patience, I utterly failed to enlighten or motivate her. I got paid for my time anyway.

Professors at University of California at Davis who brought literature to life for me, like the one who could read Chaucer aloud with all the 13th century trills and diphthongs just after he related the story of how he got a speeding ticket on his way to class in very modern English.

He usually came into the lecture hall with a wool plaid scarf casually flipped over his shoulder. It goes without saying, but I'll say it anyway: his tweed jackets had leather patches on the elbows. I cannot leave out the professors (I regret their names are gone from my memory) who made history exciting for me. Nothing like Colonial Christianity to get you going first thing in the morning!

Christie Munson Muller, my writing sister, who collaborated with me in forming Valley of the Sun Writers' Consortium, a creative group for our friends. It was at the monthly workshops that I first became familiar with Lydia's voice. Original members Jennifer Gartner, Joy Hsu, Judy Hayes, and other participants who joined us through the years, for the wonderful sessions that they facilitated in the hosting rotation with Christie and myself, and for their kind and constructive feedback on the scenes from Seeking Lydia that I shared with them.

My birthday sister, Carmanlita, told me about Tom Bird's writing program. It was at his weekend retreat in Sedona that I wrote Seeking Lydia as a novel, knitting random vignettes together and tackling the tough scenes that I had resisted writing down.

Other local writers and leaders in our creative community who have inspired, instructed, and encouraged me along the way include Amanda Owen, Leah Downing, Duane Roen, Judith Starkson, Susan Pohlman, and Windy Lynn Harris.

My second dad, Jeff, encouraged me and supported me in this endeavor, which was set aside for a few years after his passing. I know my fathers are cheering me on from beyond the veil. In fact, I feel that lots of folks on the other side have been with me, whispering insights into my ear and lending their emotions and voices through my fingers to the pages of this story. Although I took much creative license, I hope my portrayals of them are in the vicinity of close to who they were.

Friends and so many in my family have believed in me and waited, sometimes impatiently, to read my first book. I appreciate your ongoing reminders that I was supposed to finish and release it into the world.

I have many long-distance cheerleaders who regularly ask me how the book is coming and when can they read it. The time is now! Thank you all for spurring me on. My varsity squad includes my loyal heart sister Valerie Patterson who knows where all the bodies are buried, Medina Santos my brilliant writer sister who I pray will someday write something, and Linda Schilling my soul sister and fellow "none" whose crazy tales have caused me to do a double-read over the years, and whose daily ministry either keeps me reflective or tickles my funny bone, depending on the day.

I appreciate that my Uncle Jim in California gave me permission to include him in the book, and to use real names. He promised that *Seeking Lydia* will have a place on his bookshelf next to his autographed Toni Morrison books!

My local Uncle Jim has read well over 10,000 books, and aside from developmental and line editors, was the first to read my manuscript and tell me it was ready to release. That was a few years ago, and since then, he has published five of his own books! I appreciate his persistence in urging me on.

I have found true guidance in this self-publishing gig from Mark Dawson and James Blatch, whose podcast entertains and informs me every Friday, and whose classes have kept me motivated and moving toward finishing, even when I was not producing anything tangible.

Some tweaks and additions and a final copy edit done, and I am now ready to let Seeking Lydia launch, as it is: perfectly imperfect.

Family Gallery

Chloe (Gold) & Willard Jonas Blighton

Blighton Girls (L-R): Clary, Grace, Chloe, Dutch, Lydia

BLIGHTON KIDS (TOP L-R): CLARY, DUTCH
(BOTTOM L-R): HIRAM, AMY

PEETER FRANKLIN

OLIVER "OLLIE" FRANKLIN

FRANKLIN KIDS (L-R): BELLE, STUBB, LEE, VINNIE, BILLY

CYNTHIA JULIETTE "DUTCH" (BLIGHTON) & WILLIAM THOMAS "TOM" MOBLEY

MOBLEY KIDS (TOP L-R): ETHEL, MAYE, DUTCH, JOSIE, EDITH, MARGARET.
(BOTTOM L-R): LOU, RAY, KENNETH, CARL

Cousins (L-R): Belle, Lee & Josie

Pitcher Lee

The Franklins picking up Chloe and Josie at the train station in Seward, Nebraska, June 1912.

Left: Lumberjack Lee
Right: Teacher Josie

Josie & Lee

Lee & Elsie

BACK L-R: LUELLA, TOM, BETH.
FRONT L-R: JOSIE, LEE

TOM AT KRON
IN SAN FRANCISCO

BETH, NANCY, DICK, AND JIM

LEFT (TOP L-R): BETH, DICK.
(BOTTOM L-R): NANCY, JIM

NANCY, CHRISTINA, AND JERRY HUVELLE

Thank you for reading *Seeking Lydia*. I hope you enjoyed it.
I am grateful for honest reviews on Amazon.com

Join my mailing list to learn about my next novel, Seeking Anna at

chuvelle.com

You can also find more information about Lydia's family there:
Family Trees
Family Photos
Family Letters
Family Recipes